The New Generations

By Frank G. Davis

Copyright © 2020
Frank G. Davis

ISBN # 978-1-954253-51-3

9 8 7 6 5 4 3 2 1

Editing, Cover, & Layout by: solfire@phoenix-farm.com

Dedication

This book is dedicated to the memory of **Douglas Fleharty,** a long time friend who passed away almost two years ago. Doug was a non-com in the Navy during the Vietnam War, serving aboard a cruiser. After the war he moved to Arizona and became a locally well-known jazz guitarist, playing at a number of clubs in the Phoenix area. Unfortunately, Doug suffered from PTSD and had to be medicated every day. He couldn't drive, so I would pick him up and go to rather long lunches at least once a week. We shared so many stories of our lives, I felt like I was his brother. He honored me by saying I was his best friend. A day doesn't go buy that I don't think of him. I miss you Doug.

Sharing this dedication is my editor, **Trish Lewis.** Without her knowledge and considerable help, I would never have become an author. She does it all. Beside editing my writing and making suggestions on how to make the writing flow, she also designs the covers and takes finished manuscripts and turns them into published novels. As a token of my appreciation, I have turned her into a senior shuttle pilot in this book who seems to anticipate her shuttle captain's orders before he gives them. I would fly with you anytime, Trish. Good hunting!

4

Preface

The Moses was seated at the head of the Temple's large conference table watching as the room began to fill up. Seated with him were the representatives of New Jerusalem; Senior Security Priest Simon was at his right hand and Dr. John Sanborn, the head of the IT department, was at his left. Others of high rank from the New Jerusalem contingency were seated at the table. Those of lesser rank sat in chairs located against the wall behind the table.

The representatives from the generation ship *Hope* were the last to enter. They were the officers and civilian leaders; Captain David Lawrence, his executive officer, Commander Henry White, the ship's security officer, Lieutenant Commander Hiroshi Koyama, and Governor John Stewart seated themselves at the table. Their support staff also took seats against the wall. That group included the ship's chief medical officer, Commander Soo Song and Anna, the wife of Lieutenant Commander Koyama and previously a six year resident of New Jerusalem. Anna was to serve as a liaison between the New Jerusalem and *Hope* representatives.

There were approximately 50 attendees in the room, a large room which could have accommodated twice that number. It was located inside the Temple complex, next to the enormous sanctuary with a seating capacity of nearly a thousand people. The walls of the conference room were adorned with beautiful paintings of Old Testament scenes. Moses, the Old Testament Moses, was the focus of many of the paintings. The largest picture was hung directly behind the New Jerusalem Moses. It depicted a life-sized God standing next to Moses on Mount Nebo showing him the Promised Land. A shaft of sunlight was shining down illuminating the land, a land flowing with milk and honey.

Once everyone was seated The Moses stood and addressed the group.

"Friends, this is an auspicious moment when our two families will join together to become one. We of New Jerusalem welcome the representatives from the generation ship *Hope* and recognize their sacrifice in protecting us from certain destruction from the scavenger army. For that we will be forever in your debt. We welcome you all.

"We recognize this will take a considerable amount of adjustment for both of our existing communities and our purpose for meeting today is to begin our planning on how that integration will be accomplished. Later today we will meet in various breakout groups to discuss and plan our approaches but let me give a short overview.

"New Jerusalem has a population of approximately two hundred thousand people. As I understand it, *Hope* has a combined population of five thousand military and civilian personnel. Is that correct?"

Hope's governor, John Stewart, replied, "That's correct. In round numbers we have one thousand military and four thousand civilian personnel most of whom are currently living in temporary housing just outside the Outer Ring of New Jerusalem. We want to thank you for moving so quickly to accommodate our housing needs. I'm told the remainder of our people will be moved out of the ancient's lab into temporary housing within a few weeks."

"You're welcome, Governor Stewart. Our first priority is to ensure temporary housing for all your people. Our second priority is to provide permanent housing. Our first breakout meeting will have as its goal to determine the type of permanent housing required, where it is to be located and when it should be completed."

"My team has suggested we have four additional breakout meetings as follows." He turned toward a vid screen and a document was presented:

1. Determine permanent housing for *Hope* personnel
2. Evaluation of the resources available within the ancient's lab
3. Determine the structure of our combined government
4. The reformation of our religious views in light of the New Testament
5. The disposition of the POWs now being held in a temporary stockade

Once everyone had a chance to read The Moses resumed speaking. "These are our recommendations for our first priorities. However, we are open to any suggestions the *Hope* leaders have to include as any other top priority."

Captain Lawrence looked at Governor Stewart, who nodded his ascent. "Actually," said the captain, "You have come up with the same list of priorities we have. It seems great minds think the same. We agree completely with what you've suggested and are anxious to have the breakout meetings begin. Do you have a target date for the committees to report their recommendations?"

The Moses gestured to SSP Simon who nodded and said, "We were thinking a week would be a good goal to report back for all the committees. If it looks like we need more time we can adjust the timing. Is that acceptable?"

Both the captain and governor nodded in agreement.

"Then let's have a short break and then go to our assigned breakout rooms. SSP Simon will show you where each room is," said The Moses. "Meet up in fifteen minutes."

Part 1

New Generations

Permanent Housing—Governor John Stewart

It was the beginning of spring in New Jerusalem and all the farmlands were being planted. New farms were being created for the farmers from *Hope* and they were incredibly excited about getting started. Residences for the farm families would be ready soon, however many didn't want to miss the planting season so they slept in tents or under the stars while they waited for houses and barns to be completed.

New Jerusalem was located in the eastern part of the old American state of Tennessee. In springtime it was an exceptionally beautiful country. The New Jerusalem farms were located west of the city, on gently rolling lands that extended for several miles in all directions. Beyond were forests of a wide variety of trees. Sycamore, maple, birch, hickories, ash, cedar and pine all grew in abundance and provided the lumber for houses and furniture. Beautiful freshwater rivers and lakes were within moderate walking distance, full of fish for the taking. Wild game was plentiful and many of the locals couldn't wait for hunting season. Not too far away from the farms were picturesque low mountains still snow-capped in the early spring. All in all, it was a paradise we never noticed because of the war, but those of us from *Hope* were beginning to see what a blessing this place could be.

I was standing outside the Outer Ring Wall watching the construction crews working on a dozen new houses. I couldn't believe how quickly they were going up. The construction foreman told me yesterday their goal was to finish a house in a month or less. That's from the time they laid out the plan on the dirt to the time it was ready for move in.

One thing that sped up the construction process was the Beam. As house plans were being laid out, a ten-story high tower was going up in the middle of the farm land to house all the Beam equipment. A control room was built in the base of the tower. The Beam was used in tractor mode to pick up large pallets of building materials just outside Outer Ring Gate W to deposit it at the individual house sites. The Beam could easily deliver material pallets for a dozen houses in an 8-hour shift. As plumbing, heating, ventilation, and air conditioning (HVAC), electrical utilities, and power sources were needed, they magically (almost) showed up at house sites. There was little down time for the construction crews waiting on deliveries.

I learned a lot from our breakout meeting six weeks ago. It turned out there were several vacant apartments inside the Outer Ring and we were able to move all our people remaining in the ancient's lab, the old Oak Ridge National Lab, into those apartments. Many opted to stay in an apartment rather than wait for a house to be built.

The housing plan called for four types of housing: apartments inside the Outer Ring, individual homes in suburban neighborhoods outside, but close to, the Outer Ring, military housing like barracks and Bachelor's Officer Quarters (BOQ), and lastly, farm houses and barns built away from the Outer Wall close to their respective farms. This last category also included the rebuilding of any farmhouses that were destroyed or damaged during the brief war with the scavenger army.

In addition to the housing, other buildings were being constructed. These included office buildings, schools and, at the insistence of Commander White, *Hope's* XO, a gymnasium with a weight room so he could continue setting personal bests.

Lieutenant Commander Koyama also requested we include an aerobics room for yoga and martial arts training. Of course, those facilities were not built until the homes were completed. In the interim, the captain and I were using offices in the Temple next to SSP Simon's office. They were quite spacious, and the staff was extremely efficient. Being in close proximity to The Moses and the

SSP has proven to be greatly beneficial. We hold impromptu meetings as items turned up that needed immediate attention. I hoped we could maintain that close relationship once our offices were completed.

Apparently, Commander White couldn't wait for the gym to be finished. He set up his weight room on a concrete pad where he worked out at least an hour each day. Rumor had it he slept there to ensure, "no one steals my iron."

Ancient's Lab/ORNL–Captain David Lawrence

I was leading a team consisting of my crew members and security priests (SPs) from New Jerusalem. This was going to be a daunting undertaking. I had no idea Oak Ridge National Lab (ORNL) was so big. From our computer records, I knew it was the largest multi-purpose science and technology laboratory in the old United States. It was sponsored by the U.S. Department of Energy and covered many scientific disciplines critical to the generation ships. Together with the National Aeronautics and Space Administration (NASA) Glenn Research Center, they developed and produced the advanced electro-magnetic (EM) ion drive engines that propelled the generation ships at over five percent the speed of light (5% c) for over two hundred years. In addition, ORNL developed the fusion reactors and their electric generators required to power the EM engines.

ORNL also developed advanced materials for the ship's exterior to stand up to the micro-meteoroid impacts at 5% c, and produced the most advanced artificial intelligence (AI) quantum computing system that essentially ran all the systems on the ships.

The list of other contributions to the generation ships was endless, but the one I found most important was ORNL's invention of the Beam System. I had no idea how it worked, but it had proven critical to our survival in so many ways, I had no doubt we couldn't have survived the recent war without it. The Beam had a dual ability. It could function as a means for transporting people and materials to and from *Hope*. In addition, it could act as a tractor beam and pick up and deliver objects from one location to another.

Not only did ORNL produce all these systems for the generation ships, they produced spare parts for us to carry on our trip to Alpha Centauri and back and also stocked additional parts in their vast underground storage area. If our records were correct, there were possibly enough spares to build another ship, or at least improve our living conditions in New Jerusalem.

ORNL's activities were not limited to supporting the generation ships. They made many advances in power generation and storage. The last solar power cells they developed were ten times more efficient than had originally been used on the first space stations. Instead of converting only three percent of solar energy into usable electric energy, they now converted over thirty percent. They also developed self-contained fusion reactor powered electric generators about the size of a washing machine that would last for hundreds of years. Our records showed there were thousands of the solar and fusion power electrical generators available for the new houses and facilities being built.

We were at it for a week and had barely scratched the surface. We needed to be extremely careful in some places due to the deterioration of some of the underground structure. *Hope's* database indicated the underground storage area was built specifically to store the generation ship parts and any supporting equipment. That would include all types of weapons that could be used on board, or on alien planets if the need arose. Laser rifles and stun wands were two that come to mind.

The SPs tell me they think fifteen to twenty percent of the lab needed to be reinforced before we could safely begin our inventory. I've ordered this restoration work to begin in parallel with our efforts to determine what's in the readily available areas.

Before we had to scuttle our generation ship, we downloaded all the information stored in our computer systems. Those data cubes held every piece of ORNL information that existed at the time of our departure for Alpha Centauri. It was estimated The Plague began approximately ten years later. It took another 10 years for it to destroy civilization as we knew it. Our onboard data bases were updated by

ORNL for fifteen years after we departed. It provided information on where everything that had been stockpiled was located and how many items of each part were stored. Maps were also available. It should have been easy to compare the ORNL inventory from *Hope* against the parts in the lab, but it didn't turn out that way.

During the two hundred years we were gone, the labs had been raided by the good folks of New Jerusalem to build and grow the city into a place were two hundred thousand people could live and prosper. Before that, it was possible that scavenger gangs looted what they thought they could use or barter to other gangs. *Hope's* records indicated ORNL had developed nuclear weapons, warheads or various yields as well as smaller suitcase bombs and even smaller, pocket bombs. No one in New Jerusalem knew anything about the nukes.

It was the first thing we looked at and, unfortunately, several of the suitcase and pocket nukes were missing. It was suggested they might have been moved without anyone knowing what they were. Moving forward, everyone was to keep an eye out for the bombs. Another suggestion was that the Angel of Death might have carried away some of the missing nukes and used them against New Jerusalem and *Hope*. Based on what we knew about the *Hope* prisoner who had a small bomb implanted inside his body, it would seem it was one of the pocket nukes from ORNL. We really needed to account for all the nukes.

New Government Structure—The Moses

This was going to be difficult, very difficult. The people from *Hope* wanted us to abolish the theocracy that sustained New Jerusalem for almost two hundred years and establish a democracy with a complete separation of church and state. How could we possibly come up with a compromise that won't lead to chaos?

I've decided I will moderate a committee and let each side present their positions and then evaluate the pros and cons. Whatever we agree on as a final government configuration, I believe it will require a long transition period with a lot of trial and error events. From one of our side conversations with the *Hope's* governor, I know they will push for the elimination of stun wands as a form of punishment and absolutely demand we do away with stoning people for capital offenses.

My head judge, Judge Aaron, said he sees no reason for changing anything. His quote was, "If it brought peace and prosperity to New Jerusalem, why would we want to change?"

It also occurred to me that this topic and the religious topic had tremendous overlap and I was considering talking with *Hope's* governor and captain about combining the two into one group. In fact, I believed we must determine how we would move forward on religious issues before we could consider how that will impact the government. Especially, if we were going to retain any form of a theocracy.

I could see it more clearly. The first thing we needed to do was to get the complete Bible, all the Old Testament as well as the New Testament, into the hands of all the people of New Jerusalem. We needed to teach them the ways of the Messiah.

I had to lead that activity. The difficulty was I'm not that knowledgeable in the New Testament. Obviously, I needed to lean heavily on Chaplain Byron George.

THE NEW GENERATIONS

15

I leaned over my desk and comm'd my office manager. "Jeremy, I need you to get a hundred thousand copies of the Bible I received from *Hope*. Yes, I said a hundred thousand copies and I need them as soon as possible. Yes, Jeremy, the entire Bible. Also, please contact Chaplain Byron George and have him come to my office as soon as possible. No, I don't know where he is. That's why I pay you the big shekels. Try Captain Lawrence first. I'm sure he would know. Thank you, Jeremy."

Religious Reformation—Chaplain Byron George

I was on my way to The Moses' office. His office manager, Jeremy, said it was urgent and to prepare to be with him for at least an hour. This would be the first time I'd been in his office and I was a little unsettled at his call. On the other hand, this may be the opportunity I had been praying for. I whispered a final prayer before entering The Moses' office complex. I was ushered into his personal office and he greeted me warmly.

"Thank you for coming so promptly on such short notice," he said to me. "Please take a seat at the table and help yourself to the refreshments."

I sat down at the large round table, into a hand-carved chair with leather padded seats and back. I'd never imagined such a grand chair, let alone relaxing in one. Apparently, it was very good to be the leader of New Jerusalem.

He poured himself a cup of tea, took a pastry and then sat down opposite me and said, "Chaplain, I've called you here to ask for your help. It's my intention to convert New Jerusalem from the image of the old Jewish model to a New Testament model. At the present time I don't know enough of the New Testament to do that effectively by myself. If you're willing, I'd like to ask you to be my New Testament expert. If you're not willing I request you put me in contact with someone who fits that role. Please understand, I would greatly prefer you were that person."

I sat speechless for a moment before I said, "I would be honored to assist you in any way I can, Your Grace. Have you a plan in mind on how to accomplish your transition goal?"

The Moses smiled widely at my acceptance of his offer and replied, "Yes, to begin with I've ordered a hundred thousand copies of the complete Bible to be made as soon as possible. I plan to distribute them to every person, or at least every family, as soon as they are available. Next, I would announce a proclamation regarding the transition and why it is necessary, and to encourage our people to read their Bible every day. I would also like to begin what Hiroshi called weekly Bible study classes to help everyone learn more deeply, more thoroughly. My overall goal is to have everyone become a Christian by the end of the year."

Now *I* was stunned. How could I respond without squashing his enthusiasm? I took a sip of juice to delay while I considered what to say. After a second sip I said, "Your Grace, your plan is well thought out. I agree completely with the mass publication of the Bible and distributing to all of the residents of New Jerusalem. I also endorse weekly Bible study classes. Besides myself, I have several assistants well-versed in the New Testament who would be delighted to lead those classes."

The Moses raised his hand and I paused. He said, "It has been my experience that Hiroshi is among the well-versed. Would he be available?"

I smiled at him, remembering what Hiroshi told me had gone on between the two of them just before The Moses ordered him to be stoned to death. "Yes, I'm sure he would make himself available to lead a Bible study class. Might I also suggest you consider having Hiroshi's wife, Anna, and the captain's wife, Miriam, to lead Bible study classes for women?"

He seemed surprised regarding having women leaders, but then began to nod his head. "Yes, chaplain, that's an excellent suggestion. What else?"

"This may take some time, please bare with me," I said. "The Old Testament model says God selected a group of people, the descendants of Abraham, to be his chosen people. All they had to do is to be circumcised. As you know, Abraham begat Isaac who begat Jacob. One of Jacob's twelve sons, Joseph, was not well liked by his brothers and he ended up in Egypt separated from his family. After many years he became very powerful, second only to the pharaoh. When a great famine struck the land, Jacob, now called Israel, and his children, and their families, and slaves, about seventy in all, moved to Egypt where food was plentiful, thanks to Joseph.

"In the Old Testament book of Exodus, it tells how for 430 years the descendants of Israel lived in Egypt. By the end of that time the pharaohs had turned them all into slaves. Then your namesake, Moses, and his brother Aaron, by the grace of God, led them out of Egypt, ultimately to the promised land—a land flowing with milk and honey. Along the way, they received the Ten Commandments, the moral laws of how men were to interact with God and with each other. They were called the Chosen of God. If anyone didn't follow the Commandments of God, they were no longer Chosen and were taken outside the camp and stoned to death. It was an all or nothing situation.

"Your current model is based on that period of time. Punishment was plentiful even unto death. Sins were only forgiven by the sacrifice of animals and had to be done at least once a year. But that time passed after the Messiah was born. I believe the purpose of the Chosen people was to show that man cannot save himself. With specific laws and equally specific punishments they still couldn't keep from sinning. No one ever stops sinning, even the Chosen, especially the Chosen.

"I need to be clear. Everyone who has lived has to die a physical death. Being saved means being raised from the dead into an immortal body, and living forever with the Messiah and the other believers in Heaven. Just as Jesus was resurrected three days after he was crucified and now resides in Heaven.

"Here is one big difference between your current beliefs and Christian beliefs. You can't save everyone. In fact, you can't even save yourself. Most importantly, you cannot earn your way into Heaven by doing more good acts than bad ones. You are only saved from your sins by a gift. That gift is the sacrifice made by the death of the Messiah, Jesus of Nazareth, who was a man without sin. He died in place of us. And all you have to do to be saved is to believe Jesus was God in human form.

"What you have to do is to teach everyone the Gospel and let them decide if they want to believe in Jesus. If they do, they become Christians. But if they don't, you don't cast them out, or kill them. You continue to love them. Why? Because they may change their minds at some point and become believers. If they never do, it's sad, but we are not to scorn them."

We sat in silence for several minutes. I could see The Moses was processing what I said. After the pause he said, "We should not persecute those who refuse to believe? Doesn't that lead to religious freedom to believe anything they want? It seems that way leads to chaos."

"It can," I agreed. "The challenge is to find a way to avoid the chaos. On *Hope*, not all of the people were Christians, but we were all able to get along. Our lives depended on working together. As the chaplain for the ship, I needed to counsel people with other religious beliefs than my own. And I did. They all knew I was a Christian, but they also knew I didn't condemn them for their beliefs. I did my best to offer my help to everyone as best I could. Of course there were some conflicts. That couldn't be helped, but I had assistants with different religious faiths and they supported me when someone accused me of being prejudice because they were not Christian. So I know from experience we can avoid chaos. It doesn't mean our approach on the ship will work here at New Jerusalem, but I feel it is an encouraging starting point."

The Disposition of POWs—SSP Simon

I sat at the conference table in my office with two of my SPs waiting for Hiroshi and others of his security crew. We were early and were munching on snacks when they arrived, exactly on time. After greetings, introductions and the passing around of the snack tray and drinks, we caught up on some small talk before jumping into the meeting agenda. I was surprised to hear Hiroshi was offering a martial arts class three days a week for an hour each day. "With all the other responsibilities you have, how do you find time to teach karate?"

"Well," he answered, "It started out with me just doing my own workouts on the concrete pad where Commander White did his weight training. He always draws a crowd when he's lifting heavy iron, but between sets some of his admirers came over and watched me doing some katas. When I finished, a few people asked if they could learn how to do that and it grew from there. Now I have about twenty students who train regularly, my wife Anna included. Are you interested in a few lessons?"

"How much would you charge me?" I asked jokingly.

"Just buy me a beer when training's done."

One SP asked, "Can I train with you, Lieutenant Commander?"

"Sure, the more the merrier. Monday, Wednesday and Friday at 1900 hours."

"I think it's time to get started," I said. "Hiroshi, do you have a breakdown of the POWs?"

"Yes, Simon. We have a total of two thousand seven hundred fifty-two people in the stockade. The total body count for the enemy was a little over a thousand. Estimates on the number of deserters is close to five hundred. The estimate was made based on the number of weapons that were recovered and had never been fired, and were also some distance from the battle lines. One surprising piece of information was one hundred seventy-two of our prisoners are from the generation ship *Faith's* crew. We had heard less than a hundred landed safely after abandoning ship. Apparently, more than the two large shuttles landed safely. The highest ranking officer was the XO, Commander Gordon Tompkins. About half of the remainder are officers and the rest were enlisted men and women. I have a breakdown of their ranks and specialties for your review."

"That's a surprise. I think we should interrogate all of them to determine what extent they collaborated with the enemy," I said. "What about the others?"

"We divided them into two categories: organized scavenger gang members and those conscripted against their will. The majority, around two thousand, are conscripts and the remaining five hundred eighty are from the scavenger gangs," answered Hiroshi.

"How many are injured?"

"A little over one thousand total. That ranges from minor all the way to those our chief medical officer, Soo Song, says aren't likely to survive. She estimates fifty-one aren't going to make it. Ninety-eight have severe injuries and will probably remain disabled for the rest of their lives," replied Hiroshi.

"Here's what I recommend, but I want everyone's thoughts on this. First, I want every one of the *Faith* crew interrogated to find out their participation in the war effort. If any of them are responsible for the deaths of our people, we execute them. Those who resisted will be determined on a case by case basis."

"The two thousand conscripts will also be interrogated to determine their level of participation. I understand some of them fragged their leaders. Those should get a medal and invited to join our ranks. Those who claim they never fired their weapons are also invited to join our ranks, but no medals.

"Members of the scavenger gangs should be executed if they played any part in the attack.

"What I don't want is having a lot of prisoners locked up in the stockade for a long period of time. I define a long period of time as more than two months. Here are the options: We execute the really bad ones. The one's we can't determine their participation or know for sure they were not involved, we give the option to join our ranks on a trial basis only, or to be set free with the warning if we see them around New Jerusalem again, they are dead men.

"Lastly, the crew from *Faith*. Hiroshi, I would like you and your people to do an in-depth interrogation of each one of them and make recommendations on what we should do with them.

"Any questions or comments," I asked.

There were none.

<u>One Month Later</u>

<u>Permanent Housing—Governor John Stewart</u>

I stood on the walkway on the top of the Outer Ring Wall and looked to the west. All of the houses were completed, furnishings were in place and the families were moving in. The landscaping would be complete within a week. They were using the Beam to transport mature trees and shrubs from the nearby forests and transplanting them into the yards and parks.

Nine hundred suburban homes were built and divided into three subdivisions of three hundred homes each. The homes were limited to three and four bedroom models with lots of open space. Six generations of living in a tin can, granted it was a very large tin can, limits the space any one person had. When the planning committee looked at the recommendations submitted by the people who would be living in the homes, the number one request was for open space. They really didn't want to be compartmentalized any longer. This carried over to the size of the lots the houses were built on. Minimum lot size was a half-acre, maximum was one acre. The second most requests were for landscaping with lots of colorful plants and trees.

The architects who designed the houses outdid themselves. They had ten different floor plans and fifteen different façades. No façade could be repeated within the same block. It gave each house in a given block a unique look. Not to be outdone by the architect, the landscape architects had their own ideas and the yards were beautiful. Each house had rich green hybrid grass lawns in front and back. They never had to be mowed and they never changed color, even in winter when the temperatures got below freezing. They used a wide variety of native plants and shrubs that began blooming in spring and kept their flowers until the first freeze. A special force field was installed around each shrub to prevent frost damage during the winter months.

Full grown, majestic trees were excavated from the surrounding forests and transported to the yards by the Beam where they were transplanted by arborists. I didn't even know what an arborist was until I met a team of them planting the trees in the yard of my house. I had moved in only a few days before and was awakened by the sound of machinery outside my bedroom window. My wife thought we were under attack and a tank had driven into our backyard.

I ran out in my pajamas to see what was going on and a man came up to me and said he was the head arborist. I thought that was some kind of military rank. Fortunately, he quickly explained why he and his team were there. He apologized for disturbing us and said they would be finished soon. I noticed this gigantic tree behind him. It must have been three or four stories tall. I assumed that was the tree they were going to transplant. I thanked them for their work and went inside to attempt to calm my wife. She was hiding behind the door and grabbed my arm as I went in. She asked, "Who are those men?" I told her they were arborists. She looked terrified and said, "I knew they were military. Is an arborist a higher rank than a general?"

The third most frequent request was for security. They didn't want to have fenced yards (they really didn't want to break up the openness with any type of fences) yet they had just survived a war and were still very much concerned about protecting their families. A unique security system was put into place. An invisible detection system surrounded each subdivision. Anyone entering or leaving the subdivision was tracked and identified. It was similar to the old, gated communities that existed over two hundred years ago, but without the gates and walls. Any unrecognized vehicle that didn't respond to a request for why they were entering was shut down by the AI that monitored the system.

There were six streets providing the entrance and exit from each subdivision. At each entrance point was a scanner that electronically interrogated each vehicle entering or leaving. No walls, no gates, just peace of mind.

Each house had its own security system on all exterior doors and windows that automatically activated when the residents went to sleep at night. It also had a panic mode which could be activated by a coded voice command. Unfortunately, our security system hadn't yet been installed when we were attacked by the arborists.

The subdivisions were separated by about a half mile. Each subdivision will have schools, parks with ponds and lakes, and recreation centers. Those will come during the next few months. The first priority was to get people a permanent place to live as quickly as possible, and the tradesmen from New Jerusalem busted their butts to make it happen.

New farmland was opened up extending the existing crop acreage by fifteen percent. The farm houses and barns damaged or destroyed by the war were the first to be rebuilt and refurbished. Three hundred new farm houses and barns were slated to be completed within a week or two. Crops had been planted and animals were sharing pastures until the new fields matured. I spoke with a number of the *Hope* farmers and they were ecstatic about living on Earth and being able to see the real stars and feel the wind on their faces. One farmer said, "I can't believe how good it feels to be truly outside. This must be what heaven will be like."

The other facilities were still in progress, but everything planned for phase one was to be completed by the end of the month. Offices and BOQs were partially completed and personnel were already moving in. The gymnasium was completed in two days and I was so happy not to have Commander White nagging me about how small he's getting because he doesn't have enough iron to train with.

Hiroshi's martial arts classes were growing by leaps and bounds. Several new students from New Jerusalem signed up. Commander Soo Song was also offering a women's self-defense class and it looked like a yoga class would be starting up soon.

Speaking of Soo Song, she's going to be the new director of the first medical center to be built outside the wall. Staffed initially by her medical team from *Hope*. The clinic was seventy-five percent finished and opened on a limited basis. When completed, all of the medical equipment from *Hope* will be installed and made operational. The center won't be limited to military personnel. It will be open to all, but primarily to those living outside the wall.

I was absolutely amazed at how quickly the people from New Jerusalem met our needs. Not only did they perform all this in record time, it was all quality workmanship.

As phase one drew to a close, phase two would be starting up. On the ship, our total population was restricted to no more than five thousand people. You had to get permission to begin raising a family. But in New Jerusalem, there were no such restrictions. The number of pregnancies was climbing very quickly and we expected a baby boom before the end of the year. Bigger houses may be needed soon for the growing families.

Interestingly, we've got many requests from the citizens of New Jerusalem to acquire new houses. I believe it was a great idea to blend the population like that. I hope we get many more requests.

One last note. We were receiving requests for two types of advanced training. The first was for technology training in a variety of disciplines, the second for general higher education beyond the current secondary school level. Both were being considered.

Ancient's Lab/ORNL—Captain David Lawrence

The reinforcing of the walls and the ceiling of the underground storage facility at ORNL were well underway. I had a building inspector from New Jerusalem come in to inspect the damage and give us an estimate on how long it would take to repair. It took him only a day to complete his inspection. He indicated there were five separate areas that were really dangerous. I asked him to clarify "dangerous." He said when the ceiling is likely to collapse at any moment resulting in death or serious injuries he called that dangerous. I agreed.

He provided me with maps showing where the dangerous areas were located. I overlaid his map with mine that showed where all the items were supposed to be stored. The nuclear weapons were in one of the dangerous areas. I told him, "We've already begun our inventory in one of the danger zones."

He replied, "I know. One of the crew from New Jerusalem said you've already been poking around in a bad place. I'm sure a captain, such as yourself, is not going to heed my warning not to go in there again until we shore up the damage. So I've decided to do the next best thing."

He pulled a large box from a cart he was standing next to, opened it up and took out a white hardhat with a spotlight on top and a face mask in front. On the back was stenciled **Capt. Lawrence**. On the front it said, **Fearless Leader**. The inspector leaned over and pushed a small button located just above the right ear hole. A high pitched voice said, "Help me. Please help me."

By then, everyone was laughing. I slipped on the hardhat and turned to my crew and said, "Let's get to work."

I turned toward the nuclear weapons storage area and took a few steps before the inspector said, "Whoa, hold on a minute, cowboy. Wait for your crew to helmet up."

He reached into the box and began pulling out more hardhats and giving them to my crew. On the front of each hat was stenciled the word **GRUNT 1, GRUNT 2,** and so on. On the back was **God Help Me.**

After we all stopped laughing, we cautiously, very cautiously, moved into the nuclear weapons storage area. The inspector and his workers got busy setting up to repair the other damaged areas.

It took the better part of two weeks to complete the repairs. The crew that did the work took pains to be sure they didn't disturb any of the items stored in those areas. In a couple of places they had to move the stored items into hallways until the repairs were completed. Inspection of all the moved items indicated no damage had been done.

It took us three days of very cautious inspection to itemize each type of nuclear weapon and the number in inventory. Before anything else, we determined if there was any radiation leakage. Since it was apparent that some of the nuclear weapons were missing, we scanned every storage area in the lab for high radiation levels just in case something got moved into a different location. The good news was the radiation levels were all normal and we could take off the cumbersome radiation suits.

Once we finished the radiation checks, the repair crew moved into the nuke storage area and began their repairs. Fortunately, they didn't have to move any weapons. The following is the result of our inventory:

Class of Bomb Rating	Inv Quantity	Counted Missing
Air/Space Del 1-10 MT 30	30	0
Suitcase 5KT -1 MT 250	245	5
Pocket .25KT-5 KT 500	475	25

My recommendation was to get rid of the bombs in the 1-10 Megaton range. Those weapons required a missile or a bomber aircraft in order to be delivered. To the best of my knowledge, none of these vehicles exist anymore, even if they did there are no pilots or support personnel available to operate them. We needed to determine how to eliminate their potential threat.

The suitcase and pocket bombs were a different matter. Their threat was very real as demonstrated by the use of one suitcase bomb (assumed rating 0.5 Megaton) and one pocket bomb (assumed rating 0.5 Kiloton) in the attack on New Jerusalem and the generation ship *Hope*. There were four suitcase bombs and twenty-four pocket bombs still unaccounted for. We needed to determine a procedure for detecting these missing bombs and do a very thorough search for them. We also needed to determine what we should do with the bombs left in ORNL nuclear weapon storage. I recommended we get rid of them.

Religious Views—Chaplain Byron George

I stood in the entry way to The Moses' office and looked at all the books. They were everywhere. Every horizontal surface was buried under stacks of books taller than I was. There was a pathway through the stacks to his desk. I could barely see the top of his head peeking out above the books stacked there.

I knocked twice on the door jam and said, "Your Grace? Are you ready for me?"

He half stood until his eyes cleared the top of the books and said, "Chaplain! Yes, come in please. Follow the path. I've cleared a space on a chair next to my desk."

I gingerly followed the path and was half way to his desk when I detected an odd odor. Odd, yet familiar, it reminded me of the aroma of all the books surrounding me as I was preparing for my oral exams to become a chaplain. I will never forget that smell, not unpleasant, but sometimes overpoweringly strong. I always preferred real books to data cubes and vid screens. My best study technique was to underline and highlight key words or phrases on the pages of my texts. You can't do that on a vid screen. Consequently, I printed hard copies of all my text books from the ship's extensive data base.

I made it to his desk without knocking over any of the stacks and sat in the chair next to him. "So, this is what a hundred thousand Bibles looks like," I said as I smiled at him.

"Heavens no. This isn't even half of them. The rest are in boxes all over the adjoining offices and even in the basement. We're handing out hard copies of the complete Bible to each and every person who attends the services tomorrow. That's something on the order of three thousand, barely a dent in the all these piles, but my goal is to have them all handed out by the end of the week. But New Jerusalem has almost two hundred thousand residents and I would like to have at least one Bible in every house or apartment. We started the second printing today and should have them available about the time we distribute all these," he said, as he made a sweeping gesture with his arm to indicate all the Bibles. But enough of that," he smiled. "Are you ready for tomorrow?"

"Yes, Your Grace. I am," I answered confidently.

"Very good! So am I. Just to recap, there will be three services tomorrow, each one an hour long with a thirty minute break in between. I will begin with a twenty minute overview and end by introducing you. You will have the remainder of the hour to present your material. We must really stick to the schedule so we can get through all three services. Services begin at 9:00am, 10:30am and noon. I would like you to be here at 8:00am to hand out Bibles and meet as many people as you can. Then I hope you can stay around after the third service to meet some of the parishioners if you could."

"Of course, I'll be at the sanctuary before 8:00am and I'd be honored to stay after the last service," I answered. I paused, then asked, "What should I wear? On board ship I always wore my uniform with the chaplain insignia, but I can wear a suit if you prefer."

The Moses smiled warmly. "Wear your uniform, please."

He stood up and put out his hand. I shook it and said, "I cannot tell you how much I appreciate the opportunity to witness to so many people. Thank you for your trust in me. I won't let you down."

"I know you won't," he replied as he handed me a copy of the Bible. "See you tomorrow."

I went back to the BOQ making certain my uniform was presentable. I gave my dress shoes a spit shine look (they're patent leather) then set my alarm for 0630 hours. I went to the Open Mess Hall located on the ground floor of the BOQ. I took the copy of the Bible to look through it while I ate. The mess hall had just opened and I was surprised at how bright and attractive it was. They had all kinds of colorful pictures on the walls and the serving lines were moving right along. I guessed they were about half full. I think I just beat the dinner rush since more and more people came in. I flashed my ship ID at the cashier and she smiled at me and said, "No charge tonight, chaplain. Meals are free all week as part of a grand opening ceremony. Good luck at the Temple tomorrow."

I was surprised she knew who I was. I was dressed in civilian clothes and I didn't remember meeting her on the ship. I returned her smile and started to speak, but she beat me to it. "We've never met, but I recognize you from your picture. It's plastered all over the BOQ bulletin boards and tells about you preaching at the Temple tomorrow."

"Are you going to attend?" I asked. I noticed she had a very pretty smile.

"No, sorry. I've got the early shift tomorrow. I would really like to go. I hear they are giving out free Bibles. I lost mine during the trip down from *Hope*. I feel lost without it."

I took the Bible The Moses had given me and handed it to her. She looked shocked. "I can't take your Bible, chaplain."

"Of course you can. This isn't my personal Bible. It's one of the Bibles we will be handing out at the services tomorrow. I'm just handing it out to you a little early."

She was a little tentative, but reached out and took it and looked down at it for a second. When she looked up, her eyes were moist. "Thank you, chaplain, Thank you so much. You'd better hurry, your food's getting cold."

"You're welcome," I said and found a table where I could look at her as I ate. She was an attractive woman, about my age, wavy black hair and dark brown eyes. The name on her name tag was Andrea. I sighed, and ate my food.

The next morning, I was at the Temple at 0745 hours and the place was already busy. Cart after cart of Bibles were lined up by the five main entrances to the lobby area. In the lobby were wide spiral stairways on each side leading up to the three balconies. I moved across the lobby and opened one of the five doors into the sanctuary. The five doors lined up with five aisles that led all the way down to the dais. The dais was over a hundred feet wide and curved from one wall to the other. Each wall had beautiful stained glass windows. At the back of the dais was what I would call a choir loft. Men and women in white flowing robes were moving toward the loft.

I spotted The Moses standing in front of the rostrum in the center of the dais. He was speaking to a tech so I walked over to tell him I was here. He looked up and smiled at me. "Right on time," he said. "In fact you're a little early. You military men are always so punctual. Why don't you walk around the sanctuary and familiarize yourself with the layout. At 8:30 we begin letting the people into the sanctuary, so pick a door and hand out Bibles. When they introduce me, walk down an aisle close to the wall and take the stairs up to the backstage area. They'll take care of you and queue you when to come out to the rostrum.

I walked up the aisle close to the wall as the ushers propped opened all the double doors to the sanctuary. I picked up one of the Bibles from a cart and thumbed through it quickly. It was very professionally done, excellent material was used and all of the quotes from Jesus were in red type.

The choir began to sing and the outside doors to the lobby opened up automatically allowing the people to began to pour in. It started out as a trickle but quickly grew into a steady stream. I was picking up Bibles from the cart and handing them out as fast as I could. An usher on the other side of the door was doing the same. When the carts were almost empty, new carts were wheeled into position. Several people recognized my uniform and thanked me for the Bible. Others took the book without even looking at me. By 0900 hours my arms were getting fatigued.

The choir stopped and the outside doors closed. I thanked the ushers for their help and began walking up to the corner of the dais. A very pleasant woman's voice filled the Sanctuary, "Ladies and gentlemen, boys and girls, welcome to the Temple Sanctuary for this special gathering. Before we begin, please stand and join the choir in singing one more hymn."

As a thousand people stood up, I climbed half a dozen steps to the dais and slipped behind the curtains. A very attractive young woman in a long dress said, "Please follow me chaplain. I have a place for you to sit off stage where you can see The Moses. Would you like something to drink?"

I declined her offer and sat down facing the rostrum, but out of sight of the audience. The hymn ended and the voice of the woman said, "Before you sit down please greet those sitting close to you." She paused for a few seconds, then said, "Thank you, please be seated."

The noise of a thousand people all taking their seats at the same time was surprisingly loud. When it became quiet, the lights dimmed leaving an overhead spotlight illuminating the rostrum. The woman's voice continued, "It's time to begin this very special meeting. You were all given a copy of the Bible when you entered today. They are yours to keep, but please keep them close today. Now it is my pleasure, and privilege, to introduce to you…The Moses."

I watched closely as he walked slowly to the rostrum and stood waiting for the applause to die down. When it became quiet, he reached under the rostrum and picked up a Bible and raised it high into the air above his head. "All of you should have received a Bible like this when you entered the Sanctuary. It is now your Bible and I want you to raise it above your head as I am doing." He waited, since

I couldn't see the audience, I assumed they were following his instructions.

After a few minutes he lowered his arm and placed the Bible on the top of the rostrum. "Thank you. You can lower your arms now but hold your Bible in your lap. This is a Holy Book, the word of God, the entire word of God. He began moving around the dais as he spoke to them. "Two hundred years ago, the first modern day Moses founded New Jerusalem based on his Bible, a very old Bible his father had used to teach him to read. But it was more than a tutorial to teach him to read. It was a story of how God chose a group of people to be his own. They were slaves, with no say in how they lived their lives any more than a cow or a goat has any say. Then the first Moses came along. God chose Moses to lead his chosen people away from slavery to a land flowing with milk and honey. And that's exactly what he did. They became a mighty nation. Why? Because God was on their side. As long as they followed God's laws, He protected them and made them prosperous. When they didn't follow God's laws, he punished them."

He stopped talking and walked to the other side of the dais and said, "Does any of this sound familiar?" I heard a ripple of laughter from the audience.

He continued, "All of this is recorded in the first five books of the Bible. Two hundred years ago, a man who had an old beaten up, remnant of a Bible he used to learn to read, also used that book to establish where we live today. The laws and rules mentioned in those books became the basis for *our* laws and rules. And just like it said in his Bible, we became the chosen and God prospered us."

He faced off stage and said, "Turn up the house lights, please. Thank you."

He walked back to the rostrum as the lights became brighter as he picked up a copy of the new Bible. "I want you to open up your new

Bibles and go to the first five books. Put your thumb on the first page of Genesis and your index finger on the last page of Deuteronomy. If you don't have a Bible of your own look at what your neighbor is doing, or look up here at me." He lifted up the Bible with the five books pinched together so everyone could see. "What do you see? I'll tell you what you see. Those five books make up about ten percent of the entire Bible. Granted, they are an important ten percent but by not having the other ninety percent we were missing out on so much of God's word, of God's plan, of God's truth." He walked across the entire width of the dais and now was walking back to the rostrum. "Turn the lights back down, please."

"A while ago, a man came to our city in an unusual way. He came down from the sky on a sunbeam. I know how ridiculous that sounds, but it's true. During his stay we nearly killed him, not once, but twice. The second time was because I thought he was a heretic. I ordered him to be stoned to death which is the proper punishment for heretics according to the Bible we had.

"At the last possible second, just as the first stones were on their way, the sunbeam returned and the man and a servant girl who had been instructed to care for him, escaped. I had no idea what to think, other than I had messed up, badly messed up.

"During the night the sunbeam came back, but this time, instead of people coming down, it was a Bible, a complete Bible sent to me by the man and his caregiver. Imagine that. A man we tried to kill twice sent me this invaluable gift. It was the same exact Bible you have sitting on your laps.

"I've read a great deal of this gift and now I want you to read it too. There will be some changes made in New Jerusalem based on what we learn in the Complete Bible. To finish my part of the story, the man we almost killed twice was from the generation ship *Hope*. Instead of destroying us for treating one of their officers so badly, they came to our aide. They kept New Jerusalem from being destroyed, sacrificing their ship in the process. We owe them everything, our very lives. Without their aide we wouldn't have survived. I'm done, but now I want to introduce to you the religious leader from the ship *Hope*, what an appropriate name. Because of the crew of that ship we have hope for a future.

"For the rest of the service Chaplain Byron George is going to share with you some very important information from a part of the Bible called the New Testament. You will be amazed. Chaplain Byron George."

I stood up and walked to the rostrum. The Moses was waiting for me and shook my hand then walked back behind the curtain. I looked out at a thousand people staring back at me.

"Thank you for your applause. Hopefully, I can earn it by what I am going to share with you today. Please take your Bible and open it up to the first book. That would be Genesis, the page with your thumb print on it." That brought a few laughs and encouraged me to proceed. "The complete Bible is written in two parts. The first part is called the Old Testament. The Old Testament contains a total of thirty-nine books written by twenty-three different authors. Moses wrote all of the first five books of the Old Testament. The Old Testament covers a number of topics. We are not going to discuss much about it other than to say the last part is referred to as the Prophets. Prophets are responsible for a number of things, but today we are most interested in their predictions of the future. Specifically, their predictions of a Savior being born that would offer the human race the opportunity to live forever in paradise. This Savior is a very unique, special person. He is called by many names besides Savior. In the Old Testament he is called by the title Messiah. In the New Testament he is referred to as Christ. Both these words mean Savior in different languages. The Old Testament prophets began predicting his birth fifteen hundred years before he was actually born. I've been told the Bible which the founder of New Jerusalem used did not have the books of the prophets, what a pity. But God works in mysterious ways.

"The Old Testament covers the history of the world from its creation, as described in Genesis, to the birth of the Messiah. The second part of the Bible, the New Testament, covers the time from the conception of the Messiah until a hundred years later.

"Okay, hold up your Bible and with your thumb on Genesis put your finger on the last page of Malachi. Has everyone found Malachi? Good. The Old Testament has three times more pages then the New Testament. The Old Testament is important. However, to me, the New Testament is more important, critically important. It tells us how to live forever in paradise with God."

"Some of you may be wondering who is this Savior I'm talking about. What makes him so special? The bigger questions are, what is he saving us from and how is he going to accomplish it? For the rest of the service, those are the questions I will be addressing. All the answers come from the New Testament of the Complete Bible you have in your laps. The first four books are called The Gospels. That is a word from an ancient language. In our language it means Good News. These four books provide all the answers to the above questions.

"I'm going to do this in reverse order. The answer is, he is saving us from the penalty for sinning. Everyone knows what sin is, right? Just ask the nearest protector, I'm sure he can tell you all about sin. And he would be willing to show you what the penalty for sin would be. I was going to ask for a show of hands of everyone who has committed a sin and been punished, however I'm short on time so, we will move on."

He waited for the laughter to subside, then began again. "The Complete Bible tells us we sin when we don't obey God's laws. But the New Testament is more specific. If we even think about breaking God's law, it's also a sin. The Complete Bible also says everyone has sinned. 'No one is righteous, no not one.' And finally, the Bible says, 'The wages of sin is death.' So we are all doomed to die. But there is more than one kind of death, the death of the body and the death of the soul. All of us here today will pass away someday. Either by illness, accident or old age, our body will die. We can't avoid that death. But the Savior can save our souls and give us an immortal body, a body that won't grow old, won't get sick, can survive any accident, a body that will live forever with God in Heaven. Doesn't that sound like a good deal?

"There are probably a lot of people wondering how that's going to happen. Maybe some of you are thinking, 'I've been good most of the time, never been caught in a sin, never been stunned by a protector. Don't I get to go to Heaven?'

"The short answer is no. You can't be saved by doing more good deeds than sinful deeds. You can't earn your way into Heaven. Just having one unforgiven sin is enough to keep you out of Heaven, no matter how many good deeds you do."

I walked away from the rostrum. "I noticed there is large altar out front of the Temple. I assume that is for animal sacrifices. Is that correct?"

I noticed most of the people nodding their heads. "You follow the laws in Leviticus regarding sacrifices?" The heads continued to nod as I turned and began walking toward the other side of the dais, making eye contact with as many people as I could. "And do you have an annual sacrifice to cleanse you of your sins?" The nodding never stopped. I walked back towards the rostrum looking towards the balconies as I went. When I got to the rostrum, I stopped. "Wouldn't it be nice to have some type of sacrifice that would forgive all your sins, the past sins, the sins of the present and all the sins you will commit in the future? I really hope you all say yes, because that is exactly what the Savior has done."

"If I remember correctly, the animals who are to be sacrificed are supposed to be without blemish. The runt of the litter won't do. It has to be the best animal you can get your hands on, perfect in every way. The blood of this perfect, blameless animal has to be shed in order for the sins you've accumulated during the year to be set aside. And you have to shed the blood of innocent animals every year, year after year after year. To completely exonerate mankind from their sins once and for all required a perfect sacrifice. But since all of us are sinners, we are tainted. God will not accept a sinner as a sacrifice. What are we to do? Are we destined to die as sinners and never to be saved?"

I slammed my hand down hard on the edge of the wooden rostrum and shouted, "Absolutely not! God has a plan for all of us to be saved. Take your new Bible and open it to John 3:16. It's the fourth Gospel, page 1,632. When you find the verse, raise your hand." I waited for a few minutes until the majority of the people had their hands raised. "Most of you have it. Let's read this together. 'For God so loved the world he gave his one and only Son, that whoever believes in him shall not perish but have everlasting life.'"

The sound was like rolling thunder. "Look up at the large vid screens. Those of you who don't have Bibles join in as we read it again. Louder now. 'FOR GOD SO LOVED THE WORLD HE GAVE HIS ONE AND ONLY SON, THAT WHOEVER BELIEVES IN HIM SHALL NOT PERISH BUT HAVE EVERLASTING LIFE." The thunder was much louder.

"One more time. This time everyone stand up and say it like you are praising God." They rose as if they were one person. They were pointing and shouting and I turned to see The Moses coming up behind me. His face was flushed and he grabbed my hand and we all recited together, **'FOR GOD SO LOVED THE WORLD HE GAVE HIS ONE AND ONLY SON, THAT WHOEVER BELIEVES IN HIM SHALL NOT PERISH BUT HAVE EVERLASTING LIFE.'**

"AMEN, AMEN and AMEN," I shouted. I turned in time to see The Moses running back behind the curtains.

"Jesus of Nazareth, the Messiah, the Christ, the Son of God, God in human form, was born and lived a sinless life and became our sacrifice. At the age of 33 he was nailed to a cross and took all the sins of mankind upon himself. Only he was worthy to be our sacrifice. But there is more you need to know."

I realized the congregation was still standing. "Sorry, I got carried away. Please take your seats.

"When the Son of God died, he was buried in a crypt, but on the third day God the Father resurrected him. He spent forty days conversing with his followers and strangers and was seen by over five hundred people before he ascended into Heaven where he sits at the right hand of God. He has promised that he will come again and all those who believe in him, believe he really is the Son of God, will be saved. The believers who have passed away will be raised from the dead and will meet the living believers in the air as they are all taken to Heaven. Those who don't believe will live in Hell without God.

"So that is my story, I'm sure you all have many questions and we will answer them all in due time, but for today we are done. Take your Bibles with you and read them every day. I recommend you start with the Gospel of John.

"I would like to close us in prayer, please stand and bow your heads. Dear Jesus, my Lord and Master, thank you for this opportunity to share your Gospel, your Good News of salvation, with these people of New Jerusalem. I pray you open their hearts and their minds, and they come to believe in you and are saved."

"Amen."

I walked back behind the curtain to find The Moses, he was busy talking with a group of men and women. There was a small boy with them holding the hand of a woman I assumed was his mother. The boy was obviously bored and was looking around the back stage area when his eyes focused on me. He smiled and waved at me and I waved back. His mother let go of his hand to point at one of the others in the group and the boy began edging his way towards me. I figured he was about 10. He walked up to me, stopped, came to attention and threw me a perfect salute. I immediately came to attention and returned his salute. The boy said in a very serious tone. "Cadet Jenkins reporting for duty sir."

"Carry on, Cadet Jenkins. Where is your base of operations?"

"I am currently stationed at Joshua Military Academy. I'm a plebe, sir."

Out of the corner of my eye, I noticed the group with The Moses had stopped talking and were paying attention to the cadet and me. I continued, "Have you been given any demerits while on duty, cadet?"

He smiled briefly before returning to his stony faced expression. "No sir, my record is clean as a whistle."

"Outstanding, cadet," I replied. "Would you please escort me to your group? I need to rendezvous with The Moses."

"Yes sir, commander. Please follow me." He did a perfect about face and I fell in behind him as we marched the ten steps. He stopped and said, "These are my parents and their friends. We all enjoyed your presentation very much."

"Thank you, cadet. Stand easy."

I spent the next few minutes conversing with the group and congratulating the cadet's parents on their son's military bearing. As we broke up and got ready for the next service to begin, I noticed the cadet was not carrying a Bible. I grabbed a copy off a cart and quickly signed it and gave it to the boy. I gave him an order. "Cadet Jenkins, you are to read this book fifteen minutes of every day."

To which he answered, "Yes sir. I always follow orders."

I hurried to the lobby to begin handing out more Bibles for the next service. Then we did it all over again.

After the third session, I wandered around the lobby chatting with members of the congregation and answering questions. The Moses was doing the same. The reaction to our presentation was mostly positive which was encouraging, but we really only reached less than two percent of the cities' population. Of course, the first session was presented live to all the vids in the city, but we had no idea of their reaction to the message. Time would tell.

I was just about to leave and return to the BOQ, when I saw Andrea standing next to one of the outer doors. I waved to her and hurried over. To my surprise, she grabbed me and gave me a very strong hug. "You were wonderful, chaplain. I'm so glad I got to see you in person. This was the most moving experience in my life."

She told me she swapped shifts with a coworker so she could come to the last service, but she had to hurry back to the BOQ mess hall to make up the time she just spent at the Temple. I offered to walk with her and she accepted. I quickly paid my respects to The Moses and excused myself.

It took us about half an hour to reach the BOQ and I enjoyed every minute of it.

New Government Structure—The Moses

Things seemed to be going well since we merged *Hope's* people with the New Jerusalem population. Praise God for that. About five hundred people from *Hope* were now living in the apartments within the Outer Ring Wall. SSP Simon had seen to it that each of *Hope's* five thousand members, both military crew and civilians, had IDs that permitted them access through all of New Jerusalem's rings. Those IDs also allowed them to make purchases from any of the stores, shops, restaurants and pubs inside of the rings. There was a daily limit on the charges allowed except on home furnishing items. All of *Hope's* charges were grouped together and a copy was sent to Quartermaster Geoffrey Taylor for review.

With regard to law enforcement, SSP Simon met with all of the SPs and protectors and indicated citations for violations would still be given out, but we would suspend on-site punishments with wands during this time of transition. The only concession to the people from *Hope* was they would be issued a warning for the first violation, and told the next infraction would result in a citation. As the head of *Hope's* security, Hiroshi would be informed of all the warnings. All those who received citations would still have to appear before a judge.

There were some exceptions to that procedure. All of the protectors were to carry wands when on duty. They were required to use them on anyone caught participating in violent crimes, but the protectors were to cease the use of the wands as soon as the violence stopped then the perpetrators were subdued and incarcerated.

One final note on the use of wands by protectors: All wands were modified so the maximum setting was a level 5. It was decided that level 6 and above were unnecessarily dangerous.

There was some grumbling amongst the protectors on this mandate. But they were told we would carefully review all wand punishments for violence to see if a level 5 setting was adequate to stop the violent behavior.

There was considerably more push back from the judges. They were concerned we were…how did Senior Judge Aaron phrase it? Oh, yes. He said, "We will be opening the gates to chaos if we treat these vicious criminal elements with kid gloves."

We had not as yet determined the changes required in our laws and the corresponding punishments for violations. But I cautioned the judges they needed to get rid of a substantial number of our current laws. Focusing primarily on frivolous laws, I suggested a first step would be to delete half of our current five thousand plus laws and ordinances. To say the least, Senior Judge Aaron was not pleased. He used very harsh language to inform me of his displeasure. I asked him if he would like to retire from his lofty position or would he like me to remove him myself. No one is allowed to speak to me in those terms. He acquiesced, begged my forgiveness and slunk out of my office. Sometimes it is very good to be The Moses.

With regard to employment, the people from *Hope* have begun seeking work. I am very happy to say they are not only very well qualified in many different areas, they are also very industrious. At last report, over a thousand of the *Hope's* civilian population has become employed within New Jerusalem's walls without displacing any of the existing New Jerusalem population.

The numbers for farmers are even higher. Nearly, fifteen hundred farmers and their support people are actively working on new and existing farms and ranches. I've been told to expect first crops from the new farms this fall. Praise the Lord!

The military crew from *Hope* numbered nine hundred seventy-two officers and enlisted men. Many of them were directly involved in supporting ship functions. Obviously, those positions no longer exist. Captain Lawrence informed me they expect their ranks to shrink to around five hundred by the end of the year and ultimately to around one hundred fifty active military positions with perhaps as many as two hundred fifty reservists subject to recall if emergencies occur.

Once the captain has completed his ancient's lab inventory, he will establish a group responsible for placing released military personnel in the New Jerusalem work place. The ship's XO, Commander White, was asked by the captain to head up an ad hoc group to help any military personnel currently seeking employment outside the ranks. It was rumored that he respectfully declined at first, claiming it might interfere with his weight training schedule. I was told the captain suggested he might have to impound all the iron in the gym as a safety hazard and have it stored in a secure area of the ancient's lab under lock and key. The XO rethought his original decision and cheerfully accepted the assignment.

Disposition of POW's—SSP Simon

We met in my office at 2:00pm on Monday. That's 1400 hours military time. I could tell by the expressions on the faces of *Hope's* officers this had been a difficult month for all of them. Actually, it had been a difficult month for the New Jerusalem security people as well. It was emotionally draining to decide which prisoners were going to live and which were going to die.

After brief hellos, we got started. "I'd like to begin with Hiroshi's team and the status of the interrogation of *Faith's* personnel. Hiroshi?"

"Thank you, Simon. We began our interrogations with the officers, starting with the highest ranking officer, *Faith's* XO, Commander Gordon Tompkins. We then worked our way down to the lowest rank. We had only two ensigns. We have completed the interrogation of all of the surviving officers, a total of sixty-one, eleven died in the emergency infirmary due to wounds suffered in combat. We are currently interviewing the surviving enlisted personnel, but we still have about thirty more to go. Five enlisted died from combat wounds. We estimate we will complete all interrogations by Friday. We recorded all of the officer's interrogation sessions. I brought a data cube with the interrogation of *Faith's* XO. Would you like to view it?"

"Yes, we would," I answered. "I'd like to compare interviewing techniques."

The vid began showing *Faith's* XO sitting at a table. His hands were shackled and connected to a large metal ring in the middle of the table. Standing behind him, on either side of the only door in the room, were two *Hope* security men, each man armed with New Jerusalem wands. The door opened and Hiroshi walked in and took a seat on the other side of the table. He stared briefly at the XO. "For the record, please state your name, rank and the ship you served on."

The prisoner stared straight into Hiroshi's eyes and said, "My name is Gordon Tompkins, my rank is Commander and I was the XO on the generation ship *Faith*."

"How did you come to be on Earth?" Hiroshi asked.

"*Faith* was returning to Earth from our mission to Alpha Centauri. As we began orbit insertion, our ship failed. It was obvious we were going to crash so the captain ordered everyone to the shuttles in an attempt to save a remnant of the ship's personnel."

Hiroshi stared silently at the XO before asking, "Why is it the only survivors are military personnel? There were no civilians among the Angel's troops."

His expression never changed as he answered. "I'm sure some of our civilians made it to the shuttles. They could have died in the shuttles during re-entry or perhaps during The Angel's military training. The death rate was reported to be pretty high during camp."

Hiroshi took a data cube out of his pocket and inserted into the vid viewer. "Computer, play scene six."

A picture of *Faith's* chaplain appeared as he began his testimony of how the senior officers commandeered all of the shuttles for the crew and how the civilians were locked out of the shuttle bays. "Stop play," he said. Hiroshi's gaze never left the XO. And the XO's expression never changed. Hiroshi gestured to one of the guards who powered up his wand, walked up to the XO and touched him on the shoulder. There was a loud **zap** sound and the XO let out a short scream. "That's torture! You can't torture me. It's against the law."

"It's against ship's law. Look around you, do you think you're still on a space ship? You are in New Jerusalem now. Their laws not only permit stun wands, they routinely use them on their own population for breaking their laws. You lied to me. It is a crime to lie to security officers. That's why you were punished. That was just a wakeup call. If you lie to me again, they will turn up the juice on the wand and stun you again. Keep lying and the stuns keep getting stronger. If you tell too many lies the last stun you receive will fry your brain…or kill you…or both. Do you understand, commander?"

The XO's demeanor began to change. He was beginning to look unsure of himself, fear was already creeping in. "One more thing I want you to know," said Hiroshi. "We have a very sophisticated machine that will tell me when you are lying. It's never wrong. Save yourself the pain and answer my questions truthfully."

Hiroshi waited for several minutes giving the impression he was studying information on his portable vid screen. In reality, he was letting the fear grow, softening the XO up for the tough questions. Hiroshi knew he would lie again to avoid the inevitable, but in the end they would know everything they needed to know.

Hiroshi stopped the vid and then continued his report. "Within fifteen minutes, we got all our questions answered, truthfully answered. He tried to misdirect us a couple of times, but the computer assumed he was lying and the klaxon blared out an incredibly loud blast scaring everyone in the room. Unfortunately, the XO wet his pants, but we forced him to continue answering my questions until we were done. The bottom line was the XO was the true second in command to the Angle of Death. He did all the planning for the attacks on both New Jerusalem and *Hope*. The Angel of Death told him his objectives and what weapons he either already had or knew how to acquire as they began their march to the Oak Ridge area. The XO also revealed that the Angel of Death already had the nukes. Apparently when a bunch of scavengers attacked New Jerusalem fifty years ago they broke into the ancient's lab and got away with a lot of things, including ten pocket and two suitcase nukes. They stored them close by in caves and came back a few years ago and transported them to the training camp in the north. The purpose of the entire war was revenge.

"None of the Angel of Death's people even knew what a nuke was, but one of the survivors from *Faith* was a nuclear engineer, responsible for maintaining *Faith's* power plants. He told the Angel of Death about nukes and what they could do. That set them to planning the war. It was always going to be a nuclear attack.

"If the Angel of Death had not captured *Faith's* officers, or if the officers had refused to collaborate with him, it is very unlikely the war would have ever existed. The results of the interrogation of the officers is as follows: All of the senior officers, from lieutenant to commander are guilty of treason. Two of the junior officers, one lieutenant JG and one ensign, are also guilty of treason. That would be a total of twenty-two men and women. It's recommended those twenty-two should be executed by firing squad as soon as possible. Of the remaining thirty-nine, nineteen should serve life sentences. Twenty should be released with the caveat they become good productive citizens or they also will be imprisoned. I will be able to give you a similar report on the enlisted men and women no later than Friday of this week."

"Thank you Hiroshi, and extend my thanks to your team. That had to be an excruciating undertaking," I said. "Let me continue with some of my findings regarding the scavenger gangs and the conscripts. All of the members of the scavenger gangs took active rolls in the war. In my eyes, they are little more than blood thirsty animals. I'm going to recommend they all be executed. I see no possibility of any of them becoming useful members to New Jerusalem.

"As for the conscripted men and women, at the present time I see no need to execute any of them. I do need to decide what to do with them. I will pray on this and make my decision this coming Friday. The final decision will be made sometime next week by our Tribunal, The Moses, Governor Stewart and Captain Lawrence."

One Year Later

Housing & Facilities—Governor John Stewart

It is safe to say, Phase 1 has been completed, very successfully completed. Everyone from *Hope* now has a permanent place to live and work. Phase 2 is in the planning stages. It will be limited to 300 residences in a fourth subdivision.

It has been a very eventful year in all aspects of the integration of *Hope's* personnel with New Jerusalem's population. For example, a large number of people from *Hope* have gotten married. Those marriages included a significant number of weddings between *Hope* and New Jerusalem people. The two most noted marriages are between ship's personnel. After six months of engagement, Chaplain Byron George married Andrea who worked in the BOQ. It was a beautiful ceremony and I can attest that the couple is deliriously happy.

The most unlikely wedding was between Commander Henry White, the ship's XO, and Commander Soo Song, the ship's chief medical officer. Everyone thought theirs was a love/hate relationship, and truth be told, it was in the beginning. The XO's only true love was with the iron he lifted. Now that his shipboard duties were done, and the special assignments were completed, he spent most of his days, "pumping iron, lots of very heavy iron."

Soo Song, on the other hand was totally dedicated to her practice in the recently constructed medical clinic. In my opinion medical clinic' was a misnomer. It was really more like a regional hospital which also included training of new medical specialists. She had brought all of the medical equipment from the ship and was able to add new equipment discovered in the ORNL storage area. However, in spite of her exhausting work schedule, she also found time to do yoga and martial arts training three times a week. This included a once a week women's self-defense class that usually ran two hours.

The difficulties between them began when one of her assistant trainers for the self-defense class couldn't attend. She talked the XO into subbing for her assistant who was supposed to pretend he was the attacker.

Now, don't get me wrong, the XO is a very happy-go-lucky guy, a gentleman around the ladies, but when he's in the gym and in sight of more than a ton of iron, he pictures himself as the biggest and baddest gorilla in the gym. And, when it comes to lifting weights, he is, but not that time.

Dr. Song's self-defense was based on a Korean style called Hapkido. It uses an opponent's size and strength against them. When she told him to attack her, slowly at first so she could show her students the defensive technique, he dutifully complied. When she told him to attack her with full power and speed, he felt his manhood, his gorillaness, was being challenged, he didn't hold back.

He quickly circled behind her, grabbed her in a tight bear hug, lifted her high off the ground and squeezed the breath out of her, all the while screaming like some maniacal beast.

Without hesitation, Dr. Song snapped her head backwards into his face, breaking his nose and causing him to loosen his grip enough for her to bring her heel up into his groin. He bent forward and loosened his grip even more which gave her the opportunity to grab his index finger on his right hand and yank it backwards breaking his grip and that caused him to drop her to the floor. His screaming had stopped by now and she twisted away from him still holding his finger, which he tried straightening, presumably because he mistakenly thought his one finger was stronger than her four plus her thumb.

As the XO was struggling to get his hand free, she swung her foot between his legs and caught his left ankle with her instep and swept his leg high into the air, at the same time yanking his hand toward herself and downward. There were two very distinct popping sounds as the XO came crashing down onto the ground. The encounter lasted about 10 seconds.

For a few seconds all of the women students stood in stunned silence, mouths open wide. The men in the gym had stopped working out to watch what they thought was going to be an easy domination by the XO. There was no doubt they were as stunned as the women.

Soo Song quickly kneeled down next to the XO and whispered in his ear, "I'm so sorry. You rushed me and your own strength caused these injuries."

Through gritted teeth, the XO said, "Please, get me to the hospital. I'm in bad shape."

When the med techs arrived a few minutes later, two large gym rats helped the three hundred pound XO onto the power gurney and watched as they took him across the street to the clinic. The doctor went with them, still dressed in her *gi,* spattered with the XO's blood.

It turned out she had broken his nose, dislocated his index finger and fractured his left thigh bone. The last injury was probably caused when he fell hard onto the mat. He was forced to stay in the clinic for a week, but he had to stop training for several months.

You'd think there would be bad blood between them as a result of the beating he took at the doctor's hands (and feet), but nothing could have been farther from the truth.

All during his recovery, they were inseparable. Many speculated he developed a healthy respect for the woman who beat him like a drum. Other's thought she was embarrassed at the injuries he sustained during their encounter, feeling she should have had more control.

Whatever the reason, three months after he finished physical therapy they were engaged. She became his spotter when he began lifting again, and he starting taking yoga from her. He never, ever went to her women's self-defense class again.

Three months later, they were married in the biggest military wedding since Hiroshi and Anna were married aboard *Hope*.

Speaking of Hiroshi and Anna, they got pregnant as did the recently wed Chaplain George and his wife Andrea. So are Captain Lawrence and his wife Miriam. The pregnancy rate has risen dramatically during the last three months and the birth rate hasn't lagged far behind. It's estimated there will be over five hundred new births from just *Hope's* personnel alone this year. Since the ship's restrictions on the number of babies that can be born were rescinded, all childless married couples decided not to wait any longer. Married couples who had children older than five years old also decided it was time for the next one.

In searching all the available data bases on birth rates, I came across a term I think will soon resurface in New Jerusalem and apply to this generation of new children; Baby Boomers. I asked Miriam to supplement this report with her own thoughts on the increase in babies during his year.

One category of construction I forgot to mention involved a substantial sized group; that would be the enemy soldiers who were allowed to remain in New Jerusalem. Special dormitories were constructed once they were judged not to be dangerous to the population at large. This group was referred to as conscripts, people who were forced into service, but didn't participate in the attacks on New Jerusalem or *Hope*. There were two thousand men and women who were judged as conscripts. They were given the choice of remaining in New Jerusalem or leaving the area of the city and never returning.

Those who chose to leave were chipped and would not be able to pass the security gates. Those who chose to stay were also chipped, but with privileges. They were under two years of probation. They had to spend the first year outside the gates, living in the newly constructed dormitory. They were all to get jobs and be gainfully employed either on farms or businesses outside the gates. If they committed violent crimes like murder, rape, aggravated assault or molesting a child, they would be executed. For lesser violations, they would be exiled and never permitted to return. There would be no second chances or temporary imprisonment. New Jerusalem had no prisons.

For those that chose to stay and made it through the first year, they would be allowed to enter the city, but not pass beyond the Third Ring Gate. They could work and visit in the outer two ring areas, but had to return to their dormitories by 10pm. The dormitory would be locked down at midnight every night.

For those that made it through two years, they would have the same rights as other citizens. They would be re-chipped, allowed access to all gate levels, including the Temple area. They would be allowed to remain in the dormitory if they chose, but they could also acquire other housing.

The dormitory itself was not a prison per se, but it did have limitations. Those living in the dormitory were responsible for maintaining their living areas as well as the common areas used by all. Single people had studio apartments, married couples without children had one-bedroom apartment and those with children had two or three bedroom apartments. Daycare was also provided for parents who both worked.

Baby Boom in New Jerusalem—Miriam Lawrence

What a year this was. The number of marriages increased dramatically. The number of babies being born began to rise during mid-year. Now as we approach the end of our first year in New Jerusalem, the birth rate is growing exponentially. My husband thinks it's because they put something in the water that increases human lust. Whatever the reason, it seems like every third woman I see is pregnant or recently had a baby.

David and I are part of that group of new parents. Once we moved into our new house, I began dropping little hints about now would be a good time to start a family. Oh, wouldn't this be the perfect room for the baby, it's right next door the master bedroom. What would you like, a girl or a boy? We're not getting any younger, in a few years we will be too old to start a family. And on and on and on. You know, subtle suggestions.

Apparently, my nagging worked. We got pregnant. Our baby was born two months ago. Boy, has our life changed since then. Not that I'm complaining, well not too much. My captain is overjoyed with our daughter. He has been a huge help with Angelique. When he's off duty he pretty much handles everything. Not only watching the baby, but also cleaning the house, washing the laundry and cooking meals. I had no idea he was so domestic!

When my captain's on duty my women friends came over and helped out. Anna has been a Godsend. We both got pregnant around the same time. Her little boy, Jonathan, was born three weeks after Angelique. Even when she was in her ninth month, she still walked over and helped out with the baby. When I told her she should stay home and rest, she said, "I only live a block away and besides Dr. Song says I should get a little exercise every day. I also want to practice changing diapers and play with little Angelique." It was so nice having her around for those first three weeks.

While Anna visited we talked about how we could help the other pregnant women and those with newborns. With the help of a lot of other women, we formed an organization called Babies Are Us. Anna and I were surprised at how many women signed up.

Dr. Song thought it was an excellent idea and dedicated space in her clinic for meetings and daycare. She also volunteered to give free checkups for the babies in daycare. The doctor and her husband, the XO, recently announced they are pregnant too.

The last thing I want to mention is Babies Are Us is not limited to the mothers from *Hope.* When Anna and I were discussing how to put our group together, we both agreed that we wanted to include the new mothers from New Jerusalem. When we mentioned it to Dr. Song she contacted Senior Healer Johnson to see if she would be interested. She gave us a very enthusiastic Yes. Now we have two additional clinics inside the gate. We encouraged all the mothers to visit all the sites and get to know each other.

When the Tribunal was informed of our activities they presented us all with an award. Plaques were placed in all three clinics stating our contribution to the integration of the peoples from *Hope* and New Jerusalem. We were pleasantly surprised.

<u>Ancients Lab/ORNL–Captain David Lawrence</u>

The inventory of the ORNL storage facility has been successfully completed. There have been some startling new discoveries as well as quantifying the amount of well-known equipment, weapons and spare parts. I think we should initially discuss the items most important to our security. That would be the nuclear weapons. Two actions were determined to have the highest priority. The first was to determine what was to be the disposition of the nuclear weapons found in the lab. The second, what actions needed to be considered to locate the known missing nukes.

After much debate, it was decided that we should destroy all of the megaton rated bombs. For the smaller suitcase and pocket bombs, all but two of each category were to be destroyed. To accomplish this, a series of shuttle trips were planned to dispose of the weapons into the deepest ocean trench we could find.

I'm happy to report, that mission was successfully accomplished. Security teams placed the weapons into lead-lined boxes. Those boxes were sealed and loaded up on a flight of four shuttles and transported to the Mariana Trench in the Pacific Ocean. Each shuttle ejected their boxes in robo-deep-divers who delivered them to Challenger Deep at the southern end of the trench. This is the deepest point in the ocean, approximately seven and a half miles below the ocean's surface. This procedure was documented in its entirety from beginning to end has been stored on a number of different data bases.

The remaining two nukes from each of the categories have been moved off site for storage. The location of the site is classified Top Secret and available to only three people at any given time. Their names are also classified Top Secret.

Regarding the missing nukes, the ORNL inventory revealed five suitcase and twenty-five pocket bombs not accounted for. Based on the confessions of *Faith's* XO, the Angel of Death' ancestors had taken two suitcase and ten pocket nukes approximately fifty years ago in a raid gone bad. It is expected that two of those bombs were used on the attacks on New Jerusalem and *Hope* leaving one suitcase and nine pocket nukes in their inventory. An additional three suitcase and fifteen pocket bombs are unaccounted for.

I ordered Hiroshi to conduct a search and destroy mission for all missing nukes. His narrative of that activity is included at the end of my report. I'm happy to say we have successfully completed the inventory of the entire lab. For the vast majority of the items listed in my directories, we match perfectly in the physical count.

I would also like to thank the construction team for shoring up the walls and ceiling of the lab which made several important items accessible for inspection. We were able to confirm we actually have all the parts necessary to build another generation ship, not that I believe we will ever attempt to do so. That also includes a number of various sized shuttles, some with improved range, capacity and operating capabilities.

In the area of computing, Dr John Sanborn discovered startling new computer systems he calls an organic AI. He claims it has parallel processing and is a heuristic system. I have no idea what that means, but according to John it's going to revolutionize our computer systems.

Our nuclear engineering people have discovered plans for a miniaturized fusion reactor that they say could have "limitless applications." Proof testing was completed over a century ago and a few pilot reactors were built but never tested. They are going over the specs and operating instructions. They hope to begin testing in the near future.

Dr. Soo Song and Healer Johnson are very excited about a new 3-D non-invasive medical imaging machine that could eliminate the need for MRI and X-rays completely. It has a miniature model that can be hand held for field use.

A complete inventory of all this and much more will be readily available within the next few months on existing vid system databases.

Search & Destroy—Lt Commander Hiroshi Koyama

I headed up a team tasked with finding the missing nuclear bombs. We used a shuttle that was discovered in the ORNL storage area and programmed its computer with very advanced software to analyze data we received from our spy drones. We had ten drones equipped with sophisticated radiation detectors used to gather data for analysis. We departed New Jerusalem and headed north to first locate the Angel of Death's training camp. The assumption was the camp was where the Angel staged his army and equipment to begin their march to attack the city. It was anticipated they had weapons stored there as well.

From our interrogation of the captured prisoners, we determined a possible site for the camp. We had a crew of six as we departed our staging area outside the wall of New Jerusalem. Our pilot in command, Lieutenant Patricia Lewis, sat at the flight controls and finished up the pre-flight check. She turned to me and said, "We're ready to rock and roll. Just waiting on your order, sir."

"Flight control, this is Shuttle Foxtrot ready to lift, over," I said.

A woman's voice replied, "Shuttle Foxtrot, flight control, you are cleared to lift. Good hunting."

The shuttle rose vertically within the beam, rotating to a northerly course and engaged drive engines. Soon we were at fifty thousand feet, cruising at Mach 3. Our estimated time of arrival was an hour and a half. During our flight, the rest of our crew began shifting our electronics from standby to operational and running system checks. The copilot, Ensign Jack Haasis, turned to me and asked, "Care to hear some tunes, sir."

"Absolutely, ensign. What do you suggest?"

"I'm partial to golden oldies, sir. How about *Born to be Wild* by Steppenwolf?"

"That's not a golden oldie, that's dinosaur ancient. That's got to be over three hundred years old. Where'd you get a copy of that song, ensign?"

"From *Hope's* computer, sir. There was a ton of all kinds of songs downloaded onto the computer before she left for Alpha Centauri. Before we abandoned ship I made copies of a category called Really Old Rock and Roll." He loaded the music data cube and said, "Play *Born to be Wild.*"

The heavy beat of the song filled the shuttle's cabin as Steppenwolf began singing,

> Get your motor runnin'
>
> Head out on the highway
>
> Looking for adventure
>
> In whatever comes our way...

For the rest of our trip to the target area, we rocked out to ancient oldies. When we came to one part of the song, we all joined in and sang loudly,

> ...Fire all of your guns at once,
>
> Explode into space...

We slowed as we approached our target area and descended slowly to ten thousand feet. We were at a hover as we passed through twenty thousand. The pilot called out, "Tally Ho. I have a visual on the camp. It's about twenty degrees to port. Estimate five miles to target."

"Good eyes, lieutenant. Take us over the camp and hover at ten thousand feet. Kill the music, ensign." To the rest of the crew, I said, "Begin scanning for high radiation levels. We probably won't pick up anything but let's be on the safe side."

As expected, we measured normal background radiation levels. The next step was to launch the spy drones and have them begin a grid search initially centered over the camp. It took an hour to do a thorough search, but radiation levels were normal.

I had the pilot land near what appeared to be an administration building. I took the two marines as security and did a quick search for anything that could be important. While we searched, the shuttle crew reprogrammed the drones to widen their search to a ten-mile radius from the center of the camp.

It was estimated it would take several hours for the drones to complete their expanded search, but we got lucky. Thirty minutes into the search one of the analysts comm'd me. "Lieutenant Commander, we got a hit. High radiation levels two point three miles southwest of the camp."

The spy drone was hovering above the target area as the shuttle touched down. We were all dressed in radiation suits as we exited the shuttle and walked toward what looked to be a bunker. The pilot, copilot, and one nuclear tech remained on board.

One of the techs carried a hand-held rad-meter and gave us constant updates on radiation levels. The bunker looked like a two-story mound of dirt with a large, vault-like door in the middle. "The radiation level is continuing to rise as we get closer, but it's still pretty low."

When we reached the door, my first reaction was mild surprise. I thought the locking mechanism would be corroded with age, perhaps rusted shut, and be a major problem to open, but a visual inspection revealed it was in pristine condition.

Before opening the bunker door we all activated our radiation force fields to give us an extra layer of protection. Of course, the door had an electronic lock, but it looked exactly like the locks in the ORNL storage area. We anticipated this and had brought along a device called an electric can opener, it took less than a minute to open the door.

Once inside, the radiation levels rose dramatically. The good news was the bunker contained all the missing nukes attributed to the Angel of Death. We were able to seal them in anti-radiation boxes and load them aboard the shuttle. It took us a little more than four hours to transport the nukes to the Mariana Trench and then head home. We took the scenic route home, going into low Earth orbit (LEO) and a high Mach re-entry listening to ancient rock and roll all the way.

Unfortunately, finding the remaining nukes wasn't that easy.

After reporting the successful outcome from our search at the campsite, it was decided by the Tribunal that a similar procedure be used to find the remaining missing bombs. It was assumed the bombs may have been hidden relatively close to New Jerusalem. It would have been difficult for scavengers to have transported the bombs very far from the lab.

A second shuttle was added to the search efforts equipped with identical detection equipment and ten more spy drones. The search was divided into two areas; Shuttle Foxtrot was assigned to west of New Jerusalem with Shuttle Tango the east. Both shuttles lifted off a week later.

We were hoping to find all the bombs in one location, but that didn't happen. The spy drones scanned the land within a five mile radius of the city without finding anything. We increased our search grid to cover a ten mile radius from the city and left the drones on their own while we took both shuttles to five thousand feet and began quick scans of likely escape routes from the city. Fifteen miles west of New Jerusalem we got a substantial spike in radiation. I said to the pilot, "Trish, come about and slow us down, follow what's left of the road." I turned to the tech manning the radiation analysis equipment and said, "Louie, give me readouts of radiations level. We need to pinpoint the location."

"We're almost on top of it now, skipper. Radiation levels are dangerously high. Recommend we shield the shuttle now."

"Trish?"

"On it, boss. Shields are up. Oh man! Look out the windshield. We're in a dead zone."

I went forward. "You're right, Trish." In a gulch between the road and a polluted creek, there was a stretch of jet black land. Water had seeped into the gulch resulting in a scum covered pond. The edge of the pond was littered with the decomposed carcasses of wild animals that had stumbled into the death trap.

Jack, the copilot said, "The water in the pond is bubbling. What would cause that?"

Louie answered, "The pond is boiling. See the vapor coming off the surface. That's radioactive steam. There's a nuke down there and its containment field is failing. This is recent and it's getting worse. We need to get out of here and get a containment crew here before this blows."

"Jack, are you getting vid on all of this?"

"Roger that, skipper."

"Open a com channel to flight ops, Jack, and give them a sit rep. Trish, recall the drones and get us home. We need to set the shuttle down away from a populated area. I need to contact Captain Lawrence."

We passed the containment team shuttle on our way back to New Jerusalem. I later found out they dropped something they called magic goop on the pond to cancel out the radiation and retrieved the remains of two suitcase bombs. They deactivated the bombs and encased them in specially designed transport cases before taking them to meet their brothers in the Mariana Trench.

While Shuttle Foxtrot was being cleaned and decontaminated, Shuttle Tango continued to search east of the city. I hitched a ride as an observer, Marine Captain Doug Fleharty, call sign Badass, was in command. He was the stereotype of a marine officer and pilot, six-foot tall, very muscular with a piercing gaze. That gaze said in no uncertain terms, *don't ever mess with me.* While we were searching the west, Tango found seven pocket bombs all hidden in individual caves of a rocky cliff ridge about nine miles from the city. That left one suitcase and eight pocket bombs to find and destroy.

Tango had also adopted the approach of quick scanning major roads and rivers as possible escape routes for whomever took the bombs. Badass explained, "We have to go a little slower and a little lower to pick up the radiation signature of the pocket bombs, but we're still faster than the spy drones. We use the drones to cover the grasslands and forests. So far the drones have not..."

One of his analysis techs interrupted him, "Captain, I have two drones homing in on what looks like possibly multiple nukes."

The captain turned to the pilot and commanded, "Lock onto the two drones and take us down."

"Captain, the target is beginning to move," reported a tech.

"I confirm the movement, captain," responded a second tech.

"Pilot, maintain altitude. Are the drones following the target?"

"Roger that, captain," replied the pilot.

"Is the target following the road?"

"Negative, captain, not on the road...target is accelerating and climbing... it's some type of aircraft!"

"Copilot, track and record the aircraft's flight, pilot, pursue the aircraft and open a com channel."

"Captain," interrupted a tech, "the radiation signature is not from a bomb. It's from a propulsion system."

"A shuttle?"

"Unknown sir, but it's not one of ours. It has a very different propulsion signature."

I watched intently as the captain processed the information. "I think I should hail them." He glanced at me and I nodded my approval.

"Unidentified aircraft, this is Shuttle Tango from the generation ship *Hope*, please identify yourself, over."

As the captain was speaking, I said to the copilot, "We need as detailed a scan of that ship as you can get."

Instead of replying to our hail, we were met with a barrage of laser fire. "Break off pursuit, bug out now!"

The first laser bolt penetrated our shield and the hull. The pilot began a series of evasive maneuvers and was quickly out of range of the fleeing craft.

"Anyone injured?" asked the captain. His voice was calm and controlled as if he were asking if we wanted to go for a walk in the park. "Sound off."

Everyone acknowledged they were fine.

"Take her down to where the target was on the ground. I want to see if they left anything behind."

Three of us left the Tango dressed in radiation suits. We walked the area with radiation counters in hand and made a discovery. A suitcase bomb was lying in a ravine close to the landing area. "It looks like they lost something in their haste to avoid us," said the captain.

The tech said, "We need some magic goop and a containment case. The suitcase shielding has been breached."

We packed up the bomb and made it back to New Jerusalem without further delay. The bomb was transferred to another shuttle for the trip to the Mariana Trench. Tango was grounded until repairs from the laser attack were finished.

As far as we knew, there were still eight pocket bombs unaccounted for. The Tribunal suspended further search activities until more was known about the unidentified shuttle.

Reformation of Religious Views—The Moses

There have been so many changes during the last year. Over two hundred thousand Bibles have been distributed. I believe I can safely say that every family has received a Bible. In addition, six Bible Churches have been built, two inside the Outer Ring and four on the outside. Each of the three subdivisions has their own church, and one was constructed next to the conscript dormitory.

The main function of these churches was to share the Gospel. The goal was to make everyone aware of the Gospel message. Chaplain Byron George's initial message a year ago was inspirational. As a result, a great number of our population has been attending Bible studies once a week. The Temple also offers Bible studies in addition to the regular Sabbath Day service.

At the present time, the Bible study classes are really Gospel studies. The chaplain put together a one year program to hopefully cover the full meaning of the Gospel message. He also set aside time to answer questions related to the Gospel.

These classes were very popular. Each Bible church can accommodate two hundred people at each class. To keep up with the demand we've had to schedule two sessions a night, three nights a week. They were considering offering afternoon classes as well.

I arranged for the chaplain to meet me in the Temple to give my assistants and me weekly classes. Those classes were attended by approximately twenty-five to thirty people.

To reach the people who can't attend one of the Gospel classes, vid recordings of each lesson were made that can be watched at their convenience. We also provided a com feature that permitted viewers to get answers to any questions they had about any of the lessons.

I was sorry to have to report not everyone is happy with this Christian program. There was an ever growing unrest amongst people from New Jerusalem who didn't support Christianity. I believed

Judge Aaron was behind this movement, however at that point I didn't want to challenge him.

Their resistance was based on the claim that the vast majority of the people from *Hope* have brown eyes. It was a commonly held belief that all the brown-eyed people on Earth were killed by The Plague as part of God's plan to do away with sinners. They suspected the people from *Hope* escaped The Plague due to the power of Satan. They denied the crew of *Hope* had anything to do with saving the city from the Angel of Death and that their complete Bible was a fraud. They staged some public Bible burnings in the Temple plaza.

Chaplain George says we shouldn't punish these people for these actions. He reminded me that he had mentioned at the beginning not everyone would embrace Christianity. He said it is not the Christian way to punish those who don't share our beliefs. As long as they are not violent, let them rant and rave and burn Bibles. Think of them as misguided children who are afraid of change. However, if they do become violent, injure people or destroy property, they needed to be dealt with. Banish them from the city for their violence, not for their beliefs.

New Government Structure—The Moses

An interim government model was put in place about six months ago. Some features were very successful, others not so much. We had a structure where I was still the overall leader and had authority over the residents inside the Outer Wall. I had two people who reported directly to me. Governor Stewart reported directly to me and had authority over all the civilians living outside the wall. Captain Lawrence had authority over the military personnel and the conscripts. He also reported directly to me. We were mandated to meet once a week or sooner if need be. While I had the final say in all matters, I didn't make unilateral decisions. We also chose to name ourselves the Tribunal.

This structure was to remain in effect for at least two years with the ability to be modified anytime it seemed appropriate. Modifications required a unanimous vote from the three of us.

We created a new organization called Legal. It included security and courts. SSP Simon was assigned this organization. Lieutenant Commander Koyama was given the responsibility for security and Judge Aaron was assigned to manage the courts. The SSP was interacting with all three members of the Tribunal since the reorganization was put into effect. The judge wasn't enthusiastic about reporting to the SSP. He saw it as a demotion. He also didn't like having to interface with Hiroshi. I believe the judge has been afraid of him ever since the trial when Hiroshi choked him out.

One of our goals was to not imprison individuals who violate our laws. To accomplish this goal we divided violations into four categories. We agreed minor infractions could be dealt with by using the wand. However, we reduced the wand settings to minimize any injuries. It was decided a level three was the maximum setting. The violations wouldn't require a trial before a judge. Protectors were authorized to administer the wand punishment on site.

I was very pleased to announce despite Judge Aaron's objections, the judges greatly reduced the number of laws resulting in violations. Most of the ones eliminated were for minor violations. First-time major infractions, such as theft or simple assault, would use the wand at settings up to five, depending on the severity of the violation. This would require a trial before a judge. Repeat offenses would require a banishment of at least one year. The offender could apply for reinstatement after the banishment period expired.

Violent crimes such as aggravated assault, arson, grand theft, illegal possession of a weapon and manslaughter would require a trial before a judge. If found guilty, a mandatory wand setting of five would be administered immediately by a protector, and banishment from the greater New Jerusalem area for at least a year would be required. Banishment could be for life at the judge's discretion based on the severity of the violation. The offender would be immediately chipped and escorted outside greater New Jerusalem's security shields. They could apply to be reinstated after the banishment period expired.

Capital violations would require execution. There were four capital violations: murder, rape, sexual molesting of a child, and violent rioting. People charged with a capital violation would be tried in a court of law presided over by a judge. Based on the evidence provided by a security priest or equivalent, a jury of twelve men and women would determine the fate of the prisoner. A lie detector would be used to determine the accuracy of all testimony. A trial would be held within one week from the date of the violation. If found guilty, the execution would occur within twenty-four hours of the verdict. The execution would be carried out by firing squad or lethal injection.

Disposition of POWs—SSP Simon

This should be the final report regarding the status of the POWs. As a result of intensive interrogation of all the surviving prisoners from the war led by myself and Lieutenant Commander Hiroshi Koyama, we determined the fate of over two thousand prisoners.

Hiroshi and his team were responsible for the interrogation of the prisoners from the generation ship *Faith.* All of the senior officers from lieutenant to commander were judged to be complicit in planning and executing the attack on the city of New Jerusalem and *Hope.* Two junior officers were also found guilty of the same charges. All twenty-two were executed by firing squad the day after the judgment was made and approved by the Tribunal.

Nineteen of the *Faith* prisoners were recommended for life sentences in prison, but that recommendation was not approved by the Tribunal. They determined there would not be any prisons in New Jerusalem. Instead, all nineteen were banished from greater New Jerusalem for life. The remaining twenty prisoners were grouped with the conscripts.

Over two thousand conscripts were located in a dormitory outside the walls of the city. The first year of their two year probationary period was completed. Those who passed were given access inside the New Jerusalem's Outer Wall to work or shop. However, they had to return to the dormitory by 2200 hours. Approximately two hundred violated the terms of their probation and were banished. A few tried to appeal the ruling while the others left the area. I was surprised only ten percent of the conscripts violated probation. I was expecting a much higher percentage. Perhaps that shows the vast majority of people would rather be part of a community than be isolated in the wastelands. Only time will tell.

Part 2

New Challenges

10 Years Later

Rear Admiral David Lawrence

A lot has happened during the last decade. The most significant was the passing of The Moses. His passing was totally unexpected and came without warning. One night, after the Sabbath service, he went to his quarters. He joked with one of his security priests who worked the late shift in the outer office. The SP said he looked and acted completely normal. He had his aide order him a light meal for dinner and it was delivered to his quarters fifteen minutes later by another aide who confirmed there was nothing noticeably wrong with him.

SSP Simon was beside himself with grief, which quickly transitioned to anger. He was positive this was an assassination. He had the remains of the meal checked for poison, he ordered an immediate autopsy, grilled all of the Moses' staff followed by those who opposed The Moses' stand on Christianity.

He went to the rest of the Tribunal and demanded martial law be enforced until the assassins were found. The remainder of the Tribunal, Governor Stewart and I, informed him The Moses had designated him as the interim replacement if anything ever happened to him. It was a temporary assignment.

The SSP's reaction to the news was not unexpected. At first, he was completely stunned by the news. "Why would The Moses choose me as his replacement? I'm not a politician; I'm a police detective, a chief of police at best. I would have thought he would have chosen one of his assistants or a judge, not Judge Aaron of course."

I responded to his rhetorical question. "He thought you were the best qualified for this type of situation. He fully expected you would conduct a thorough investigation of his passing, leaving no stone unturned. You have been authorized to spend up to ninety days to determine the cause of his death. You will also be expected to assist us in determining his replacement. Whoever is chosen will serve to the end of The Moses' term, two years and four months from now."

"Excellent," he replied. "I want to declare martial law until I determine who assassinated our beloved Moses."

There was a poignant pause before Governor Stewart spoke. "Simon, I think declaring martial law at this point is premature. I would suggest a two pronged investigation. First, have the doctors determine his cause of death. Second, assume it was an assassination and fully investigate that possibility. Simon, you are the most thorough investigator I have ever met. If it was an assassination, I have every confidence you and your staff will find out who is responsible. If it is one or a few misguided persons, they will be executed. I would recommend we revert to stoning in this instance. The stoning pit is now a museum, but we could get it opened for this special occasion. If it turns out to be a coup, then I think martial law would then be certainly required."

I added my thoughts to the governor's. "I agree and I believe security for the three of us and the Temple should go into effect immediately. What do you think, Simon?"

Simon sat silently for a moment; his eyes closed. He took a deep, ragged breath, let it out slowly and said in a voice laced with pain, "You are right of course. I am no politician, but I am an exceptional investigator. I will do my job as you described. I will be patient. But when we find those responsible for his death, I will be the one to cast the first stone."

Governor John Stewart

Greater New Jerusalem changed significantly over the last ten years. As Admiral Lawrence stated, the death of The Moses was the most critical, however the city and surrounding suburbs underwent a substantial growth spurt in spite of our loss.

Within a new Outer Wall, we now had two ten story buildings, one for offices and the other for apartments. Our civil engineers selected locations for both buildings that were not on top of the ancient's lab. Fortunately, due to the growth of the city, a new Outer Wall expanded the city limits and gave them more sites to choose from. When the plans for the suburbs outside the wall were being made, those plans allowed for city growth.

Speaking of the suburbs, two more communities of three hundred houses each were built to handle the increase in population. We are now close to two hundred fifty thousand inhabitants. Of course, the increase in people required more schools, churches, hospitals, stores, and recreational facilities.

Something called golf has become all the rage. It was considered great exercise for older folks. It required a lot of land, something like an enormous park with beautiful landscaping. There were lakes, called water hazards, and sand traps. The object of golf was to hit a small ball with a club as far as you can while avoiding the water hazards and sand traps onto a small, fairly flat surface called a green. I don't think that's a very good name since the whole golf course was comprised of green grass. Somewhere on the green was a small hole, called a cup. There were nine or more different little holes. It usually takes three or four hits to get the little ball into the little hole in the green. However, for beginners it could easily take twice that many hits.

The first golf course had nine different holes. However, due to the popularity of the game, we had three new golf courses built, each with eighteen holes. The new golf courses added running tracks between what were called fairways. The land between where you first hit the little ball and where it goes into the little hole in the green was called a fairway. The last golf course built also had a bicycle path around the entire course.

When the courses were covered in snow during the winter, another sport called cross country skiing became popular. Narrow wooden slats called skis were strapped to your feet and you slide along the course on top of the snow. It's not as easy as you think it would be. I was told it was a lot of fun.

When all these new activities were presented to our Director of Recreation, Commander Henry White (retired), he didn't appear overly impressed. He commented, "All this new stuff is geared towards having fun, not building strength, or speed or power. Not very many people will want to do these things. I think our resources could be better used to increase out weight rooms and aerobic and yoga training areas."

Fortunately, after a brief discussion with his wife, Medical Director and Hope Hospital President, Soo Song, he relented and signed off on the golf courses.

One thing we didn't planned for was the influx of immigrants. More and more people wanted to become residents of New Jerusalem. Our Tribunal held a number of town meeting to discuss and determine how to deal with the immigrants. Instead of unilaterally deciding, the Tribunal held an election of the residents to determine their preference. A lot of people thought this was a bad idea because it set a dangerous precedent. They were used to having a leader who dictated these types of issues. The Moses presented the position that to be truly fair, we needed to let the citizens have a say in how they were ruled.

The Tribunal was very pleased with the results. Almost eighty-five percent of the eligible citizens voted. They chose to treat the immigrants like the conscripts. Two thousand enemy conscripts from our last war had been housed in dormitories for a two year probationary period before they were accepted into the city. That probationary period was over eight years ago. The dormitories were being used as temporary storage since then. Of the two thousand conscripts, almost three quarters completed their probationary period and were granted unrestricted access to the city. The other quarter either decided not to stay or were judged guilty of violations and banished for life from the city and the suburbs.

The vote permitted two thousand immigrants to move into the dormitories immediately on a first come first served basis. They were required to follow the same rules as the conscripts with a couple of changes from the conscript's original rules. Whenever an immigrant was judged to have committed violations to the agreement and were banished, a new immigrant would be allowed to replace them. It was anticipated two hundred to three hundred would be banished each year based on the performance of the conscripts.

Every year, two thousand additional immigrants were allowed to enter into the program. New dormitories facilities would be constructed as needed.

Of course, there were some skeptics and nay sayers, and some modifications were required, especially during the first two years. During the first two years there were more than two thousand immigrants applying for entrance, but after that, it slowed down. It stabilized to about a thousand per year applying.

A big concern by the detractors was the type of people we were allowing to join us. Were they scavengers, or malcontents, or people with no useful skills to contribute to the city?

After ten years we were happy to say the detractors were proven wrong. The vast majority of the immigrants were so grateful to be given a chance to improve their lives, only a very few had to be banished. Tracking the longevity of their accomplishments showed after ten years a substantial percentage became very successful and contributed substantially to New Jerusalem.

The Church—Chaplain Byron George

It was an arduous ten years for the Church. The death of The Moses only a few years into the decade resulted in catastrophic consequences in its growth. The Moses was the rock on which the transition from Judaism to Christianity was based. With his death, the movement faltered as if it were dying too.

After a prolonged period of grieving, a slow recovery began. People began to return to church services. Attendance at Bible study classes steadily grew, but everything had a feeling of sadness associated with it. What finally pulled us out of our depths of despair was the revival.

The Moses had chosen two young men to become his apostles. He was grooming them to become leaders in the church after he was gone. Little did we realize how soon that would be. These were the two men who accompanied The Moses from the Temple on that fateful Sabbath evening. They were called Brother Paul and Brother John. Both men were very intelligent and quickly grasped the Gospel message. Perhaps even more important, they could explain the Gospel in such a way the message was readily understood by people of all ages. They put together a training syllabus for team teaching the Gospel. The Moses had high praise for their efforts and was going to begin having them demonstrate their methods to other Gospel instructors when he was murdered.

The brothers approached me a few months after The Moses' funeral and suggested something called a revival would help get us back on track. I had never heard of a revival. I learned it was also referred to as a camp meeting or merely a gathering. I hadn't heard of those either. They explained they accessed some old vid files that described a popular way of bringing everyone together for a week or two which focused primarily on our religious beliefs. There was singing of hymns, prayer sessions on a variety of topics, guest speakers and Gospel teachers. It was like a group vacation away from the city. We would eat together on picnic tables with a military-like serving line, sit around campfires at night to share our religious experiences, sleep in sleeping bags under the stars, and grieve as a group for those who passed on.

I had reservations about their suggestion, but it was certain we needed to do something to get us out of our spiraling depression. A month later, in early fall, we held our first camp meeting. It was successful beyond all my expectations.

It ran for five days, the weather was chilly, but dry. The cool weather caused the trees to turn. We had a kaleidoscope of bright red, orange and yellow leaves interspersed with evergreens. We held the gathering at an existing campsite on a nearby lake. It was too cold to go swimming, except for the hardier of us, however, canoeing was a lot of fun. During breaks between our sessions we had time to just get close to people. Most of us were Christians, but not all of us. We invited everyone who wanted to come, no restrictions.

We planned for two hundred people to attend. To be on the safe side we prepared for three hundred. We were very pleasantly surprised to see a little over five hundred show up, at least for a day or two.

One thing we had not planned for were the farmers. They had just finished harvest and asked if they could set up a farmers' market on the edge of the campground. They volunteered to provide all types of fresh fruits and vegetables as well as eggs, chicken and beef. My wife, Andrea, got some of her friends from the BOQ mess hall to assist in preparing food for all the meals.

I know this may sound corny, but we felt an outpouring of love building throughout the entire week. Many of us, including my family, didn't want that feeling to end. We vowed to carry this love for each other forward, and never forget this feeling.

For the next five years we've had similar gatherings. The popularity grew tremendously, and we had to add more gathering weeks to accommodate all the citizens who wish to attend.

Last year we expanded to five one-week gatherings at the end of summer and into the fall, almost three thousand men, women and children attended. The Tribunal decided to honor The Moses and named the last gathering of each year, The Moses Christian Gathering.

Growth & Conflict–Brothers John & Paul

To begin with, we are brothers, twins actually, as well as brothers in Christ. John and Paul were not our given names. They were the names The Moses gave us when he chose us to be his disciples. That was almost ten years ago. He said the word disciple meant students. We were to be his students. He would be our teacher and mentor.

A year before his passing he said we were no longer his disciples. We were now his apostles. The foreign word apostle means messenger. We were now expected to speak on his behalf, teach Gospel lessons to adults and children, and preach sermons to the congregations.

At first, our assignments were to do our teaching and preaching separately. This was done at the Gospel churches and missions throughout the city and suburbs as well. It was almost a year after we began our new mission, we were allowed to take part in the Sabbath services in the Temple.

One day, after about two months of observing our efforts, The Moses said to us, "I want you to try something different. Instead of teaching separately I would like you to teach together. I think you would be more effective as a team. I've noticed you have the ability to finish each other's sentences when you are together. You do it flawlessly, as if you were one person. I have noticed twins seem to have the ability to do this quite often. However, you two take it to a whole new level, as if you are mind-linked. It's very effective in holding your audience's attention. I believe it also seems they retain more of what you say."

We began experimenting with our team teaching and preaching at a Gospel Church in one of the suburbs. Instead of one pulpit there were now two, separated by about ten feet. The mics were set up to split the speakers in the sanctuary. When Paul spoke, his voice came from the speakers on the left side. When it was John, his voice came from the speakers on the right. When we spoke in unison, our voices came from all the speakers. We did one dry run with the sound techs in an empty sanctuary and felt comfortable. We were ready. Or so we thought.

We chose as our sermon topic: **What is the Value of the Ten Commandments for Christians.** We had sort of rehearsed our sermon and felt very comfortable, until we noticed The Moses invited the entire Tribunal, Chaplain George, all the senior officers from *Hope*, and all the elders from the Temple. It was a full house.

The choir finished their last hymn. We stepped up to our respective pulpits. John said, "Happy Sabbath, church." His voice plainly heard on the right side of the sanctuary.

Then Paul immediately repeated, "Happy Sabbath, church." His voice also heard plainly, but to the left of the church. Then we said in unison, "Happy Sabbath, church. There was a slight delay with Paul's speakers which gave an echoing effect.

"I'm Apostle John," said John.

"I'm Apostle Paul," said Paul.

In unison, without the echo, we said, "We would like to welcome you to the first Team Preaching event ever held in New Jerusalem. We ask the congregation to stand as we come to the Lord in prayer."

In unison we said, "We are going to divide up the congregation with the left side saying the prayer along with Apostle Paul and the right side with Apostle John. Watch the vid screens if you are confused.

Apostle Paul	Apostle John
Our Father who art in heaven	
Hallowed be thy name.	
Thy kingdom come	
	Thy will be done
On Earth	
	As it is in Heaven.
Give us this day	
	Our daily bread
And forgive us our debts	
	As we forgive our debters.
And lead us not into temptation	
	But deliver us from evil
For thine is the kingdom	
	And the power
And the glory	
	Forever and ever.
Amen	Amen

It was a little rough at first, but everyone got into it with a rousing Amen at the end.

After everyone was seated, we continued in unison, "Today's sermon is about the Ten Commandments given by God to Moses at Mount Sinai. Moses and his brother Aaron and his sister Miriam led over a million Israelites from slavery in Egypt. Their first stop after crossing the Red Sea was at Mount Sinai where they camped after escaping the pharaoh and his troops."

Paul said, "God had Moses ascend to the top of the mountain where he gave them the Ten Commandments, ten laws, on how they were to behave toward God and how they were to behave toward each other."

John picked it up, "The Israelites had been slaves for centuries and did whatever their Egyptian masters commanded them to do. Once they were free, they had no idea how to behave. Without the Commandments of God, things would have turned to chaos in a short order."

Back to Paul. "Moses had been at the top of mountain for weeks and the Israelites became unruly. They gave Aaron gold they took from the Egyptians and had him make an idol, a golden calf, for them to worship. They threatened Aaron with death if he didn't do as they ordered."

John added, "When Moses finally came down from the mountain and saw many of the Israelites worshipping the idol he was incensed. He threw down the stone tablets of God's laws breaking them into pieces. He gathered the idol worshipers and had them killed as a sacrifice to God and to teach the remainder that God would not be mocked."

Paul finished up the topic, "God called Moses back up the mountain and gave him another set of stone tablets. The Bible says the laws were inscribed on the stone tablets by the finger of God. When Moses came down the mountain again it was said he glowed with the glory of God and men could not look at him. That glow faded and Moses called the Israelites together and read all the commandments to them. The first four described how they were to act toward God. The remaining six described how they were to act toward each other. God, speaking through Moses, promised the Israelites if they obeyed his laws, they would become a great nation and would inhabit a land promised to Abraham over four centuries before, a land flowing with milk and honey. However, if they did not follow the laws there would be serious consequences."

"Take a look at your bulletin," said John. "We have printed out the commandments and arranged them into the first four on one page and the last six on the next page. Keep these for reference. The commandments are recorded in the book of Exodus, beginning with chapter twenty."

We went through all ten of the commandments one at a time. It was a review for most of the congregation, however, it was new to a few. We also went over the penalty for breaking the commandments. There appeared to be only one penalty: death by stoning. If two witnesses observed anyone committing a sin, they would go to Moses or Aaron and tell them what they saw. Moses or Aaron would then have the offender taken outside the camp and it was the responsibility of the Israelites to participate in the stoning. There was no executioner.

The Old Testament records the first violation was for a man gathering wood to build a fire on the Sabbath. He was stoned to death the same day. One man was stoned for disrespecting his parents in front of witnesses. Justice was swift. People were stoned for murder, stealing and adultery. Initially, all that was required were two adults who were present at the violation to tell Moses or Aaron and they would order the stoning immediately.

Paul added, "That was the way it was over two thousand years before the birth of Jesus. The question before us today is whether these commandments are still in effect. Some say we are no longer under the law because Jesus died as an atonement for our sins, for all our sins. Atonement means to make something right when you have done wrong. Instead of being stoned to death for our individual sins, Jesus told Father God he would die in place of us. We would still die a physical death, however, if we believe that Jesus is God in human form, we would live forever in heaven with him and all those who believe."

"What about those people who claim to believe but continue to sin?" asked John.

"If you truly believe Jesus is the son of God, you will do your best to not sin. Jesus said, 'If you love me you will keep my commandments,'" answered Paul.

"What about those who say they have never sinned?" interrupted John again. "I have never killed anyone or stolen anything or committed adultery. Why do I need a savior to die for me when I'm such a good and holy person?"

Paul slowly turned his head to look at his brother with a frown on his face. "You lie," he said gruffly. "Don't forget, I'm your brother I know exactly what sins you have committed. That lie is just one more sin."

John answered indignantly, "I beg your pardon. I never broke any of the commandments. No not one."

"No not one. Doesn't that sound familiar? If I remember correctly another Apostle Paul said, 'No one is righteous, no not one. All have fallen short of the glory of God.'"

"That can't be true!" John whined. He looked as if he was about to burst into tears.

"Jesus said if a man thinks about stealing another man's property, if he lusts for his wife, hates him because he is rich, he is guilty as if he committed theft, adultery and murder," replied Paul. "In God's eyes, the thought is taken as the deed. We are all sinners and we need a redeemer. Fortunately, we have one. His name is Jesus."

John hung his head in mock humility, "I guess you're right, brother, but do we need to keep all the commandments?"

"The answer is yes, in thought as well as deed. We are to love our brothers and sisters and love God with all our heart and mind and soul," answered Paul.

John raised his head and smiled at the congregation. "Please pick up your Bibles and open them to Matthew 5:17 through 19." He waited for a few seconds then said, "Please join us in reading these very important verses spoken by our Savior regarding the law."

The congregation rose and began to read aloud:

> Do not think that I have come to abolish the Law or the Prophets; I have not come to abolish them but to fulfill them. I tell you the truth, until heaven and earth disappear, not the smallest letter, not the least stroke of a pen will by any means disappear from the Law until everything is accomplished. Anyone who breaks one of the least of these commandments and teaches others to do the same will be called least in the kingdom of heaven, but whoever practices and teaches these commands will be called great in the kingdom of heaven.

"That is the message we want to leave you with this Sabbath. The Ten Commandments are still in effect. The penalties may have changed, but not the moral laws," said John.

"The ideal we should set as our goal is to love one another. Because if you love one another you won't kill or steal or do all the other things the laws forbid. You won't even consider being sinful when you love each other like true brothers and sisters in Christ," added Paul.

"In our future sermons, we will look at each of the Ten Commandments and discuss them in more detail," said John. "Remember this as you leave the church, we are all sinners and will continue to be so all our lives, but with the help of Jesus we can become better Christians. We can sin a little less each day and love a little more. In your prayers, ask the Lord to increase your faith and to guide you down the path of righteous living. Thank you all for coming. May you have safe journeys home."

There was a brief meeting with the Tribunal, Chaplain George and some of the Temple Elders. To our very great relief, they were all pleased with our sermon, not only the content, but also the team preaching approach. Chaplain George suggested we repeat the sermon at the Temple next Sabbath for all three services. The Tribunal suggested we have the services recorded and made available on vid for those who couldn't attend one of the Temple services.

They also agreed on taking each one of the commandments each Sabbath for ten weeks in a row, delving deeply into the meaning of the law and its present day application.

We'd already started preparing sermons dealing with the first four commandments and were very excited about covering all ten. This was more than we'd ever hoped for.

We felt truly blessed.

We were not prepared for the resistance we encountered both from within the church and from without. We feared instead of unifying the church it might lead to a schism. We needed to move carefully, but we were not willing to compromise on what we considered to be core values.

Divisions Within—Chaplain Byron George

It was critically important that we first defined our core values. These values won't be compromised under any circumstances. In the Christian Church we believes there were five core values.

Number One: The Bible is the Holy Word of God. Everything written in the Bible was inspired by God and is without error. It was written in two testaments: The Old Testament and the New Testament. The Old Testament covers the time from creation up to the birth of Jesus, approximately four thousand years. The New Testament covers from the birth of Jesus up to the death of the last apostle, Apostle John. It covers almost one hundred years.

Number Two: God created the heavens and earth and everything that is in them. Life did not evolve from nothing. It was created by God. The writing in the book of Genesis describes creation.

Number Three: God is one person, comprised of three entities. There is God the Father, God the Son and God the Holy Spirit. These three entities are called the Trinity. They are referred to throughout the New Testament. Each has a specific mission.

Number Four: God established a moral code called the Ten Commandments. It is written in the Old Testament in the book of Exodus and again in Deuteronomy. In the New Testament, Jesus says in the book of Matthew that the Ten Commandments define sin and will continue to be valid until the end of time. Jesus added one commandment just before he was crucified. He said, "Love one another as I have loved you."

Number Five: The only way to Heaven is by believing Jesus is truly God in human form. He is the Son of God. He died as a sacrifice for all our sins. Three days later, he was restored to life in an immortal body. All those who truly believe that, and keep his commandments, will live with him forever in paradise. There is no other way to Heaven. Salvation cannot be earned.

These five beliefs summarized our core values. Once The Moses, the last to hold that title, passed away he left behind a legacy of transition from a type of Judaism to Christianity. His strength of character held us together during the change. Now that he was gone, some of the Christian beliefs were being challenged.

I would like to address one challenge that involves the fourth commandment. I am sad to say that the people from the generation ship *Hope* were responsible for the dispute.

The fourth commandment says:

> Remember the Sabbath day by keeping it holy. Six days you shall labor and do all your work, but the seventh day is a Sabbath to the Lord your God. On it you shall not do any work, neither you, nor your son or daughter, nor your manservant or maidservant, nor your animals, nor the alien within your gates. For in six days the Lord made the heavens and the earth, the sea, and all that is in them, but he rested on the seventh day. Therefore, the Lord blessed the Sabbath day and made it holy.

Most Christians worship on Sunday, not on the Sabbath. When we were onboard *Hope,* Christian services were held on Sunday, Jewish and Muslim services were held on Saturday, also called Sabbath.

When asked why we worship on Sunday, the usual answer is that we were celebrating the resurrection of Jesus from the dead, three days after his crucifixion on the cross, Sunday morning.

The Moses questioned me about this shortly before this death. He said he could find no Biblical justification for changing the day of worship and asked if I could help him research when, if and why the change was made.

We asked the twins, Paul and John, to assist us in doing a database search. They found a rather obscure document entitled **Sabbath Versus Sunday**. It was written several hundred years ago by an unknown author. In it, he summarized how the Christians changed the day of worship.

It all had to do with Roman persecution. In the middle of the second century AD, the Roman emperor Hadrian hated the Jews. At that time, Christianity was considered a sect of Judaism. Most of the persecution took place in the city of Rome and it was quite severe. Anyone worshiping at a Jewish Synagogue on the Sabbath was tortured and, in many instances, put to death.

The leader of the Christian church in Rome at the time, Bishop Sextus, took it upon himself to distance the Christians from the Jews and decided to change the day of worship to Sunday. To justify this unbiblical move, he said it was better for Christians to worship on Sunday to honor the resurrection of Jesus. He believed Christians were not subject to the Jewish laws and customs.

This change of worship days was primarily limited to the church in Rome and many Christians opposed it. Their argument was that God ordained the Sabbath as a holy day of rest and worship. No man had the right or the authority to change a decree of God.

Fast forward two hundred years and the Christian church was still divided on their day of worship. When Constantine became emperor of the Roman Empire, he denounced the pagan religions and converted everyone in the empire to Christianity. The vast majority of the pagans in Rome were sun worshipers and used to worshiping on Sunday. To ease the unrest of the pagans during their transition to Christianity, and since many Roman Christians already worshipped on Sunday, Constantine made Sunday the official day of worship for all of the Christian churches. By the end of the fourth century Roman law forbid anyone to worship on the Sabbath. It also decreed that the Sabbath was no longer a day of rest.

The information presented in the paper was quite surprising, but not compelling enough to offset over two thousand years of tradition. After all, we had no way to authenticate the pronouncements of the unknown author. Fortunately, the author cited his references for his paper. One was extremely significant. It was a doctorate dissertation on the same topic entitled ***From Sabbath to Sunday, A Historical Investigation of the Rise of Sunday Observance in Early Christianity,*** by Samuele Bacchiocchi. Dr. Bacchiocchi was awarded a gold medal from the leader of the Catholic Church, Pope Paul VI, for graduating with the academic distinction of *summa cum laud*. We were not able to find the book on *Hope's* database, but Dr. John Sanborn was able to reconstruct a partially corrupted copy from the ancient's lab. It was in much greater detail than our paper from the unknown author, and very compelling.

We presented our findings to the Council of Elders, a group of over five hundred men. Their recommendation was that we worship on the Sabbath, but for those who couldn't accept the ruling, a limited Sunday service would be permitted.

The Tribunal met and voted unanimously to approve the Elder's recommendation. Four months after The Moses' death, it was put into practice.

<u>The Autopsy–Rear Admiral David Lawrence</u>

The Moses' autopsy was conducted in the New Jerusalem hospital, very near the to the Temple complex. It turned out to be the same hospital Hiroshi was confined to when he came to scout out the city. I thought it strange that he asked to be present during the procedure. However, he had observed more autopsies than any other *Hope* security personnel and wanted to confirm it was done properly. He smiled and said to me, "I don't remember much of when I was here. It won't be a problem."

Chief Senior Healer Johnson and Dr. Soo Song were the lead physicians, with a very large staff of doctors and nurses to assist. There were so many observers as well as medical staff, they scheduled the autopsy in a teaching theater with a balcony that surrounded the table. All non-essential personnel were required to observe from the balcony. Simon and Hiroshi were the only non-medical personnel present in the operating room.

Before the team began, the SSP and acting Tribunal member spoke. "This is the most important autopsy you will ever perform. Don't think of this as a common autopsy. Instead, think of this as a delicate surgery. Everything needs to be done properly. We can't have anything done that contaminates potential evidence. Anytime samples are taken to the lab, a security officer or protector will accompany the lab technician who is making the delivery. Once in the lab, the security officer will observe and record the analysis. Everyone needs to pay special attention to following correct protocols. I believe this could have been an assassination not a natural death. No one is to reveal this information outside of this room. Everything will be recorded and reviewed. Do I make myself clear?"

There was a general nodding of heads.

I introduced Chaplain George who said a prayer before the procedure began. After that, it was all business. I observed from the balcony for a brief period. I had seen several autopsies during my career, but I couldn't tolerate seeing a man I respected and loved cut apart. I left the OR and headed for my office with my new security team in tow.

Several hours later, Hiroshi and Simon joined the governor and me in the Tribunal conference room. Simon looked terrible and Hiroshi didn't look much better. Simon spoke first. "It was an assassination. I knew it in my gut. He was poisoned by a fast acting neurotoxin. It was almost undetectable. Dr. Song said it was a designer poison created to kill almost instantly then mutate into something very similar to non-toxic saliva."

"How did they detect it?" asked the governor. "He'd been dead for over eight hours. I would think the poison would have all mutated to saliva by then."

"It had," answered Hiroshi. "There were multiple tissue and fluid samples collected and analyzed. There were several saliva samples analyzed and a tech noticed one batch that was slightly different than all the others. He pointed it out to his boss who ignored him saying there were always some variations in composition of body fluids and told the tech to disregard it. Fortunately, the tech decided to run it through some analysis machine that works at the molecular level. The first pass said it was not human saliva and it was still in the process of mutating. The tech ran the analysis again and asked it to determine its original composition."

"They can do that?" I asked. "They can reverse engineer the mutation?"

"Admiral," answered Hiroshi, "I have no idea how this worked, but the tech and his boss were very sure of the results. The machine spit out several possible compositions, but the one it assigned the highest probability to be correct turned out to be a neurotoxin."

The governor asked, "Do you know how it got into The Moses?"

Simon answered in a menacing tone of voice, "Not yet, we are working on it and will keep you informed. Once we find out how it was administered, the next step is to find who made it and who gave it to him. I can't wait to find out."

Senior Security Priest Simon

I devoted my life to finding the murderers of The Moses. I delegated all of my other responsibilities to a few of my SPs. The remainder of my staff joined me in the investigation. We began our efforts with how the neurotoxin ended up in The Moses' body. Was it in his food? Was it injected? Was it in the air? How about by touch? We brainstormed all the possible ways The Moses could have been infected. The list was quite long. We attempted to prioritize the possibilities, but felt we needed some experts' perspectives. We started with the two doctors.

"Thank you for joining us, doctors," I said as I greeted them at the door to our conference room. "Please come in and have a seat. Thank you for taking time from your busy schedules. We'll do our best to get through this as quickly as possible."

"How can we help?" asked Senior Healer Johnson.

"We need to determine the most likely way the poison ended up in The Moses' body. Before we begin, I need to caution you both to not discuss this with anyone outside this meeting. We have not announced his death was an assassination. We don't want the assassins to find out we are onto them."

"We understand Simon. We will only discuss it between ourselves," answered Dr. Song. "We anticipated you would have questions regarding the neurotoxin. Senior Healer Johnson and I had some discussions, very private discussions, as to how The Moses was poisoned. We agree it is highly unlikely an airborne delivery system was used."

"Why is that?" I asked.

Senior Healer Johnson answered, "The neurotoxin doesn't become active at room temperature. The activation temperature needs to be in access of ninety degrees Fahrenheit. If it was mixed with air from the ventilation system, it would take very large dosages and would have left a residue of inactive neurotoxin on all the surfaces of the room. We checked The Moses' office and found no such residue."

"Could he have been injected with the poison?" I asked.

"We don't think so," answered Dr. Song. "During the autopsy we went over every inch of The Moses' body looking for any puncture marks or signs of a pneumatic injection and found nothing. Each one of us did it independently and both of us came up negative."

"Could someone have blown the poison into his face?"

"No Simon," Dr. Song replied. "We checked that out too. There would have been a concentration of residue in his nasal passages and throat if that approach were used. It wasn't present."

"How about in the food or drink, or some form of coating on the utensils?"

"That was our first choice," Senior Healer Johnson answered. "There was no residue of either the neurotoxin or the synthetic saliva on anything. We even checked his bathroom and had his toothpaste, water glass, and floss checked. We found nothing."

I sat back and tried to think of any other way he could have been poisoned. I couldn't come up with anything else. "Anyone have any other suggestions?"

"Sorry Simon. Nothing else comes to mind. If we get any new ideas, we will let you know," answered Dr. Song sadly.

Commander Hiroshi Koyama

I met with Simon and a few of his SPs and protectors to review the vids of The Moses' movements before entering his office for the last time. Ever since the Tribunal was formed, a special level of security bots monitored each of them whenever they left their offices. These bots were airborne drones, very small and almost silent. Most of the time, they went unnoticed, unless a threat was perceived. At that time, they became very apparent and positioned themselves between the threat and the Tribunal member. Loud verbal warnings were made continuously until the threat was contained. At the same time, an exceptionally strong electronic shield would be activated. If the bots determined a proactive approach was needed, they attacked the threat and a level eight stun was administered.

Normally, five bots track each Tribunal member until they entered their office or residence. Other security measures were employed at those locations. However, a minimum of two bots continued to monitor the Tribunal member at all times.

On the night of his murder, the Moses left the Sanctuary after the final Sabbath service and walked with two of his apostles down the connective hallway to the elevator at the Temple offices. They exited the elevator and walked fifty feet to the offices. Two of his bots stopped there and hovered on either side of the doors. The remaining three bots entered with him and his apostles. After a brief conversation with an SP, he spoke to his aide to order his dinner and then entered his quarters where he remained until his body was discovered the next morning. When he entered his quarters, one bot remained hovering at the door and the last two followed him inside.

Fifteen minutes later, another aide brought his dinner on a power cart. The aide entered the Moses' quarters, transferred the food from the cart to his table, then left.

That was the last time anyone saw The Moses alive.

I assigned two security people to review the vids from each bot. There were also seventeen surveillance vid coms at fixed locations in the Sanctuary lobby, hallways, elevator and Temple offices. There were no security vid coms in The Moses' quarters or private office.

I assigned two security people to review all fixed vid com recordings as well. I decided to sit in on the review of the data from the lead bot. It was one of the two that entered The Moses' quarters.

It took over two hours to complete the review. Each team was to review the time period from when The Moses left the Temple sanctuary until he went into his quarters. Those reviewing the activities in his quarters were to continue reviewing until the time of his apparent death. Team members were not permitted to discuss the results of their reviews until we were all present in the Temple conference room. We also invited SSP Simon to attend our debriefing.

Simon made some introductory comments before the debriefing began. "I want to thank all of you for conducting reviews of the bot vids and facility vids. I look forward to hearing the results of your efforts. I consider this the most important part of the investigation. I expect to come away with strong leads as to who murdered our beloved Moses. Please begin."

We began with the reviewers of the facility vid coms. As expected, there was nothing of any significance to report until The Moses and the two apostles arrived at the Temple offices. It was pointed out no physical contact was made between The Moses and either apostle. They hardly spoke. The bot vid reviewers made the same reports including the short trip in the elevator.

When The Moses paused to speak briefly with the SP there was nothing out of the ordinary to report. While in the office area, no one touched The Moses, and no one did anything out of place.

These reports verified what was expected. But the expectations were very different once The Moses entered his office. The two security bots covered his every move. They recorded him changing out of his ceremonial robes and into his pajamas, and then slipping on his bathrobe.

When the aide arrived and placed his dinner on the table, one bot recorded the aide's activity up until the time he left The Moses' quarters. Special attention was given to the aide to determine if he placed anything on the food once it was set up and the dish covers were removed. Again, nothing suspicious was observed.

When done, the aide guided his food cart out the door. He paused briefly to wish The Moses a good evening and then left closing the door behind him. The second bot was focused on The Moses while the aide placed the food on the table. He appeared to be reading some church documents. Once he finished eating, he retired to his bedroom, sat in an easy chair and began reading his Bible. One bot accompanied him into the bedroom and the other took up position in the office area where it could view everything from the balcony to the bedroom door.

The scans were fast-forwarded through the next two hours. Once he finished reading the Bible, he took care of his bathroom needs, kneeled down at the foot of his bed and prayed, rose from his prayers, turned out the light and went to bed. During those two hours he didn't appear to have any discomfort.

Once the lights were out the bots' changed to infrared imaging. They also went into motion detection mode. The bot in the office became active an hour later. A pale blue light shown from the balcony and a man appeared to beam down. The intruder opened the balcony door and entered into the office. It was difficult to see the intruder's face in the dim light as he made his way to the bedroom as if he were familiar with the office layout. Once inside, the other bot became active.

The intruder said, "Computer, activate bedroom lights, low setting." The voice sounded familiar. He sat down in the easy chair next to the bed, removed something from a small satchel he was carrying, and reached over to touch The Moses' shoulder to wake him. "Your Grace, please wake up. I must speak with you. It's very important."

The Moses stirred and opened his eyes. "Oh, it's you. What are you doing in my bedroom at this hour? Is there an emergency?"

"I'm afraid so, Your Holiness," he answered as he stood up with the object from his satchel. "I want you to know I admire you above all men I have ever known. Without your guidance New Jerusalem would never have become what it is today. However, it is time for you to go."

"Go? Go where?" There was no fear in The Moses' voice, more like inquisitiveness. "Should I get up and get dressed?"

"No, Your Grace, just close your eyes, lay back and relax. It will only take a moment."

As The Moses reclined then closed his eyes, the intruder put what looked like an oxygen mask attached to a small canister over The Moses' nose and mouth and said, "Breathe deeply, Your Grace." A low hissing sound could be heard as The Moses took a deep breath. The intruder turned off the canister, removed the mask and placed it back into the satchel. He looked down at The Moses and noticed his eyes were partially open. One tear had made its way down his cheek. He leaned down and kissed the tear; you could hear a sob coming from the intruder. He stood up, turned to leave the bedroom and faced directly toward the security bot. He made no attempt to hide from the camera.

The intruder left the bedroom quickly and walked onto the balcony. The blue-white light shone brightly for an instant as the beam carried him up and away from the Temple.

There was stunned silence throughout the conference room for a moment, and then I stood and faced SSP Simon and said. "Senior Security Priest Simon, you are under arrest for the murder of The Moses."

The Tribunal Review—Governor John Stewart

The next morning, the Tribunal met in the small conference room in the Temple offices. Rear Admiral David Lawrence was present, and Judge Aaron had been asked to sit in as a temporary Tribunal member. Commander Hiroshi Koyama had called the meeting and the three of us waited for him to make an appearance. When he entered the conference room, he was followed by SSP Simon in shackles with two large protectors as escorts.

Judge Aaron jumped to his feet and shouted, "What is the meaning of this? Why is SSP Simon in chains?"

Commander Koyama answered him, "Because he has been charged for the murder of The Moses."

All three of us said at the same time, "He's what?!! That's impossible!"

Hiroshi raised his hand for silence, and everyone waited to hear his explanation. "I know what you are thinking, 'There's no way Simon killed The Moses.' Unfortunately, we have vid com data that shows it happening, even though I don't believe it either. I had him arrested and isolated until we could all meet together. As the next highest ranking government member of New Jerusalem, I invited Judge Aaron to take the SSP's place on the Tribunal.

"Before we go any further, I want to show everyone the vid com evidence. Computer, play bot one vid data segment F."

The vid screen at the end of the conference table came to life with a picture of The Moses' Temple office. The view was in infrared until a blue-white light shone on the balcony. We all watched in muted shock as the scene moved to the bedroom and the killing of The Moses and to the unmistakable view of SSP Simon leaving the bedroom and being beamed up from the balcony.

We were all stunned by what we had just seen. Hiroshi was the first to speak. "I believe the vid is a fraud. First of all, I checked with the beam techs and they corroborated that our beam was on stand-by status for three nights surrounding this incident for routine maintenance. So, if the murderer beamed down, he didn't use our beam. Secondly, both Dr. Song and Senior Healer Johnson said the neurotoxin could not have been injected by the mask pictured in the vid. It would have left a residue in the Moses' nasal passages and throat. The autopsy revealed no such residue was present. Finally, I would bet every last shekel I have that Simon is the very last person on Earth who would have killed The Moses. Besides, he has an alibi for the evening in question. He was playing poker with the admiral and me at the time of the murder."

Rear Admiral Lawrence asked, "Where do we go from here?"

Hiroshi answered, "First, quarantine everyone who was involved with the vid review. Let them know they are not allowed to speak of this with anyone, the official secrets act and all that. Make them aware they will be punished with a level eight stun if this information leaks. Let them all know there is sufficient evidence to suggest the vid account we saw was a fraud. We are examining it and will keep them informed of our findings. Secondly, make a public announcement The Moses' death was by natural causes and hold a funeral fitting for someone of his stature. Lastly, figure out how he was really killed and who did it."

Simon had sat quietly during the entire meeting. I asked if he had anything to add. He shrugged his shoulders. "I want to continue to lead the investigation," he answered in a flat monotone voice. "No matter how long it takes, I will not rest until we have solved this murder and my name is cleared. I believe I was chosen as the patsy because we were getting close to identifying the real killers. Thank you all for your confidence in me."

The meeting ended and Simon was escorted to a secure facility to continue his investigation. He requested Dr. John Sanborn join him, at least for the foreseeable future to determine if the vid was a fraud, and how they hacked our security bots. We knew this was going be a lot more difficult than the vid hack the Angel of Death used prior to our war several years ago.

Commander Koyama reminded me there was still the alien shuttle we encountered during our search for missing nuclear bombs. We still had made no progress to identify where they were from and why they fired on us.

Hiroshi said, "I have this gut feeling The Moses' assassination and the unknown shuttle are somehow connected."

Senior Security Priest Simon

My IT specialist was waiting for me in our secure facility when I arrived. I smiled at him. "Very punctual, Dr. Sanborn. Are you ready for a new challenge?"

Dr. Sanborn didn't smile back. In fact, he looked rather sad. "I will do everything I can to prove the vid was a fraud. I just hope it's enough. May I view the incriminating vids?"

"Of course, doctor. I see you've brought your overnight kit," I said as I loaded the security bots' data into the vid com. "It's ready to play, but please excuse me if I don't watch it again. I'm beginning to get a migraine headache from watching it multiple times. I'm going to lie down on one of the cots. Please wake me if you have any questions."

I took some pain medication given to me personally by Senior Healer Johnson who assured me it was not poison. Ten minutes later, I was fast asleep. According to Dr. Sanborn I was having some violent dreams. I awoke with a start after falling off my cot. I was dreaming I was at the stoning pit surrounded by hundreds of people ready to throw their stones. Just before the first stone hit me, I realized they were all me. I was stoning myself. When I fell to the floor, I thought it was the first stone striking me. I woke up screaming.

John was at my side in an instant and helped me up. He guided me to a chair and handed me a glass of water. I sipped slowly as the spinning room slowed down and finally stopped. He watched me quietly and waited for me to speak first.

"How long was I out?" My voice sounded like a croaking frog. I cleared my throat and asked again.

Dr. Sanborn answered, "Almost two hours. I've finished my preliminary reviews."

"What do you think?" I said, not sure if I was ready for his report.

"First the bad news, this is the most sophisticated fraudulent vid I've ever seen."

"What's the good news?" I was beginning to feel panic and added, "There is some good news, isn't there, John?"

"Of course, Simon, there's a two second gap between the bot vids. When the intruder entered the bedroom there was an overlap of vids between the two bots. Based on the time stamps the intruder entered the bedroom two seconds before he opened the door. It's a minor point, but I still consider it significant. One other point concerns the light from the beam. It appears it originated from the side of the balcony, not from overhead. It would have to come from above for the intruder to both enter and exit the balcony.

I swallowed hard as some of the tension left my body. "Good work, John, in fact, excellent work. You're off to a good start."

"One last update; I believe the intruder was real, but they gave him your face and voice. It's like they somehow deactivated all the passive alarm systems in The Moses' office and bedroom, yet they kept the security bots recording so it would appear you were the murderer. It's going to take some time to unravel all the details. Whoever doctored the vid coms and hacked into the bots have very advanced equipment, perhaps more advance than ours."

The New Presence—Commander Hiroshi

I started with the data from the mystery shuttle that attacked Shuttle Tango while we were searching for the missing nuclear bombs from the ancient's lab. There was a lot of data to review. I recruited Marine Captain Doug Fleharty, call sign Bad Ass, to assist me.

We had done a cursory look at this data some years ago, but we never saw the intruder shuttle again. We did a very extensive search of the immediate area, and then widened the search area to include everything within a hundred mile radius of where it fired on us. Nothing remotely promising was discovered. We began looking for possible motherships in low-earth orbit using *Hope's* astronomical search hardware installed on the top of the beam tower. Again, it was a dead end. After several months, the search effort was downgraded to a very low priority, essentially discontinued. Nobody was comfortable with the decision; however, there were too many other more pressing problems. The good news was we found the missing pocket nukes and disposed of them with the others in the Mariana Trench.

Doug and I brained stormed possible new search methods. One he mentioned sounded promising. "We haven't found a trace of the shuttle. To me that leads to two possibilities. Either it is hiding out in a very sheltered hanger a long way from New Jerusalem or it high-tailed it to an orbiting mothership."

At first I protested. "We already ran three months of scans for orbiting ships and found nothing."

Doug smiled, an unusual expression for a man called Bad Ass, and said, "What if it's in a high synchronous orbit on the other side of the Earth, or at least far enough away from us that we can't detect it."

I thought for a moment before shaking my head. "I don't think a shuttle would have enough power to climb to a twenty thousand mile orbit. LEOs are usually only a couple of hundred miles above the surface. That's about the limit for our shuttles."

"Maybe *their* shuttles are jazzed up," replied Doug. "I went over the data when they escaped from us. Their acceleration rates were twice what our shuttles can manage. It might be worth a look."

"How can their crew handle such a high acceleration rate? If we tried that we'd be smeared all over the deck plates," I countered.

"Maybe they have robotic crews instead of humans or maybe they have super inertia dampeners to control the G loads," he suggested.

I smirked at him. "Inertia dampeners? Really? I think you've been watching too many old science fiction vids. If they have robots or inertia dampeners their technology is generations ahead of ours."

"You got any better ideas?" he said in a challenging voice.

"No, not really," I answered. "How do you recommend we go about it?"

"Take one of our large shuttles, strip out everything we don't need for the mission. Install reaction mass bladders to give us more endurance. Reprogram the flight control computers for sustained LEO. We'd need some instrumentation to detect a mothership in a synchronous orbit. Seems like a piece of cake to me. If one's out there we should be able to detect it in a couple of orbits, no more than five, at ninety minutes per orbit we'd be done in eight to nine hours. What do you think?"

"I seriously doubt it will be a piece of cake." I paused and then said, "What the hell. Let's do it. Take care of getting the shuttle reconfigured. See if we can install some firepower and stronger shields. Let me know if you find any inertia dampeners."

A week later, Shuttle Sierra was ready for takeoff with a crew of eight. The Tribunal had given their approval and we were strapped in and ready to launch.

Trish, piloting this mission, contacted New Jerusalem Flight Control, "Flight Control this is Shuttle Sierra requesting lift off. Over."

"Roger, Sierra, Flight Control, expect beam lift off to launch in ten seconds. Good hunting. Over and out."

Trish, in her command voice, said, "Hope everybody is strapped in, lift off in five, four, three, two, one, lift."

The tractor beam grabbed the shuttle and began lifting it vertically off the pad. It was a two G lift and accelerated the shuttle to nearly five hundred miles per hour as the shuttle passed through an altitude of three thousand feet in less than five minutes.

Jack, the copilot, was monitoring the shuttle's propulsion system and giving updates. "Reactor to max power and holding, reaction-mass pump at one hundred percent. Ready for launch in five, four, three, two, one, launch."

As soon as the tractor beam disengaged, Jack pressed the launch button and the shuttle's main propulsion system came online. Trish pushed the throttle forward and the thrust quickly ramped up to maximum. When the tractor beam disengaged the shuttle went from two Gs to weightless for only an instant. When the shuttle's propulsion system came up to max power, the crew was subjected to five Gs as the shuttle accelerated to orbital velocity.

It had been several years since I'd been exposed to five Gs. I was glad I had continued to weight train along with the karate practice. It really helped manage the G forces. As mission commander I monitored the crew's biosuit readouts and was happy to see everyone was within the safe range.

When we reached orbital velocity, the main engines shut down and we became weightless again. Even though the crew were seasoned spacers, it had been awhile for all of us, it was great to be in space again. I did a quick check, "Sound off. Any problems?"

Everyone reported they were okay, "Let's get busy, crew." I began reading off the checklist of getting the shuttle prepped for at least five orbits. The first thing we did was to make sure our shields were at full strength. LEO is a junk yard of orbiting debris which could potentially damage or even destroy the shuttle. More importantly, nobody had forgotten how easily the intruder's lasers cut through our shield and hull the first time we saw them. Fortunately, back then we were in the atmosphere and no one was injured. If they breached our hull now, while we were in orbit, we'd all die. We beefed up our shields by a factor of three. Hopefully, that would be enough to ward off any attack.

In addition to the shields, we installed offensive weapons of our own. The ancient's lab had some very sophisticated rapid-fire pulse lasers. Bad Ass demonstrated the lethality before we installed them on the shuttle. The demo was very impressive, to say the least. We also carried ten missiles with high explosive war heads.

The most important new feature was the detector equipment we hoped would let us find a mothership in a synchronous orbit. It was set to differentiate a mothership from the remnants of the telecommunication satellites which were also in the same orbit. Of course, none of the telecom sats continued to function. They'd all become derelicts over a century ago.

Before we completed our first orbit, all systems were operational. We began our hunt for a mothership.

Marine Captain Fleharty had responsibility for flight operations including defensive measures. I was in charge of the techs as they searched for this mothership. We'd completed two orbits and had mapped all of the derelict comsats. It was surprising how many we found. On the third orbit we struck gold. There was a sudden flurry of activity by the techs, a lot of yelling back and forth in tech speak. Louie, the tech leader, pumped his fist up and down three times and said excitedly, "Tally ho, we found it! We're recording data now!"

Doug heard and pushed off a bulkhead and floated towards us. "What's up? You found something?"

I answered, "Louie says they spotted the mothership. I can't wait to see their inertia dampeners."

During our next orbit we reviewed the data collected on the mothership. It was big, but not as big as a generation ship, maybe only half as large, with a much sleeker design. It didn't have a rotating barrel to produce synthetic gravity. It was unlike any ship we had seen before. I asked Louie, "Have you checked data bases to identify this ship?"

"I did that first thing. Nothing concrete showed up," answered Louie. "The only thing remotely close is a top secret file that alludes to an advancement over the generation ships. It's called the coffin ship. I don't have the capability to open top secret files up here."

I turned to Doug and asked, "How long before we are in com range of New Jerusalem?"

Captain Fleharty checked his data pad and answered, "Twelve minutes. Once we get are in range you have twenty minutes to get a return message."

I turned back to Louie and said, "Put together a burst message to Dr. Sanborn at New Jerusalem with everything you have on the mothership. Ask him to crack the top secret file. We need information on the ship's mission, performance, defenses and offensive weapons and we need it within fifteen minutes once he receives it. You've got ten minutes to get the message together and laser burst it to Dr. Sanborn, highest priority. You copy?"

"Aye, captain. I copy and will comply."

While the techs began another flurry of activity, I took Doug aside and said, "I'd like to get a closer look at the mothership, how about you?"

"Absolutely, captain. I didn't come up here for the beautiful view. Let me check to see if we have enough reaction mass left to get us to synchronous orbit and then back to New Jerusalem."

Dr. Sanborn replied with two minutes to spare. The mothership's mission was almost identical to ours. They were to travel to Proxima B, an Earth-like planet orbiting the star Proxima Centauri, four light years from Earth. They were to drop off more colonists and upgrade the existing colony. That's where the similarities ended.

The coffin ship was designed to operate at twenty-five percent of the speed of light, five times faster than our generation ships. That meant it would reach Proxima B in about twenty years instead of taking the hundred years our generation ships needed. That takes into account the time it took to accelerate from orbital speed to twenty-five percent of the speed of light, and then decelerate to orbit at Proxima B.

The ship used a new propulsion drive system based on magnetohydrodynamics, MHD for short. It was supposed to be significantly more advanced than the EM drive we used on *Hope*. A new, very advanced, shielding system had been developed to deflect micrometeorites in the ship's flight path. When larger particles were detected, computer controlled laser cannons would reduce them to dust. We couldn't find information on the firepower the canons could produce. That was considered a major concern if we decided to approach the ship. There was no mention of any inertia dampeners.

The relatively small size of the ship was due to the way the passengers were accommodated. The ship could transport up to five thousand passengers in boxes referred to as coffins due to their shape. They could've come up with a better name. They were actually cryogenic-sleep containers. Everyone, including the crew, would be placed in cryo-sleep as soon as the ship left Earth's orbit and remained that way until they were revived just before entering orbit around Proxima B. The ship was completely controlled by a triple redundant computer system that took care of life support for all the coffins as well as flew and navigated the ship to its destination.

While in cryo-sleep, the passengers were kept in a state which simulated hibernation. This dramatically reduced the aging process; the passengers and crew aged a year during the twenty year trip. Nutrients needed to sustain life were fed intravenously.

The construction of the ship began after The Plague started, but before it became a pandemic. It was built by a consortium of European countries. As The Plague began to spread worldwide, the passengers and crew were quarantined in Earth-orbiting habitats until construction was completed. There were delays and for a while it appeared the mission wouldn't be carried out; eventually they launched.

That was the last information available on the mothership.

There was no record of the trip or if they accomplished the mission. All we knew for sure is that they were now in synchronous orbit around Earth and one of their shuttles had fired on us.

What should we do next?

The Coffin Ship–Marine Captain Douglas Fleharty

I knew immediately what I wanted to do. However, I wasn't sure if we had enough reaction mass to do it. I quickly said to Hiroshi, "I want to go to the coffin ship. We need to determine if we have the reaction mass to get there and back. We can't pass up this opportunity."

Hiroshi smiled and answered, "I'm with you." He turned to the flight engineer and asked, "Darin, can you determine a way to intercept the coffin ship and still get us back to New Jerusalem? Do we have enough reaction mass?"

Darin smiled too. Everyone wanted to see the mothership up close and personal. "I can give you an answer in fifteen minutes, skipper. I assume you want to get us home before our life support runs dry."

"That would be a most correct assumption, lieutenant. Carry on. The clock's ticking," answered Commander Koyama.

In twelve minutes, Darin had our answer. "We're a go for the coffin ship. I included a ten percent contingency for reaction mass and life support. That way Trish won't have to dead-stick the shuttle from LEO to New Jerusalem. More importantly, we won't have to hold our last breath all the way home."

I shook my head, suppressed a smile and said to Darin, "Now I see why your call sign is Joker. How many days will this take?"

"The plan calls for twelve hours to check out the coffin ship. Total mission time estimated at two days, ten hours, and thirty seven seconds," answered Darin with a grin.

"Is that a rough estimate, lieutenant?" asked Trish.

Still grinning, Darin shook his head and answered, "Nothing I do is rough. It's always smooth."

"That's quite enough," I said sternly. "It's beginning to get deep in here. When do we leave LEO?"

Darin looked at his wrist chrono, "Nine minutes, fifty seven seconds and counting."

I looked over at Trish. Before I could ask, she said, "Course program locked into the flight computer. Reactor will engage in three minutes and reaction mass pump in two minutes after that. Suggest we all sit down and strap in. We'll be at two Gs for a while."

The trip to synchronous orbit was uneventful. We engaged our defensive screens just as we left LEO. It provided us with protection as well as some degree of stealth. We really didn't want to be detected by the coffin ship and have them start shooting at us as we climbed the gravity well. To enhance the appearance we were random space junk we shut down our propulsion system several hours away from the ship and continued a ballistic approach that wouldn't take us so close as to be considered a threat.

We shot past the aft end of the ship and then fired retros to keep us close enough to scan it. The scans came back negative. The ship appeared to be abandoned, a derelict waiting to be salvaged.

We located the shuttle bay doors on the aft port side. They were wide open. As Trish maneuvered and began our approach, the crew finished suiting up in their environmental gear. By the time we touched down, we were all ready to go exploring.

We exited Shuttle Sierra and split up into three groups of two. Our pilot remained on Sierra with one of the two marine guards. Even though the ship looked abandoned we needed to be able to bug out if company came calling. Trish set up a continuous scan of the space between Earth and the ship. If she detected any inbound traffic, we were going to beat it back to our shuttle and get out of Dodge as fast as we could.

One obvious thing was the empty shuttle bay. All the shuttles were gone. Judging by the size of the bay they had ten or eleven shuttles in all.

120

Hiroshi and Joker headed for the bridge, while the rest of the crew flew to various parts of the ship. It had been a long time since I had been in a zero G environment and I found myself bouncing off the walls as I headed to the propulsion room. Our helmet vids recorded everything we saw and said as we made our way throughout the ship. In addition, everything was transmitted to New Jerusalem in real time just in case we didn't make it back. I was sure Dr. Sanborn and his analysts were already pouring over the data.

During the next twelve hours we checked everything. Any hardware that we could repurpose was confiscated and stored aboard our shuttle to be investigated upon our return.

Darin made an incredible find. The ship was controlled by a triple redundant computer system. When he attempted to explain it to me, assuming I was interested, it was as if he was speaking a special tech language. I think he realized this when my eyes glazed over. Apparently, each of the three computer systems was located in different parts of the ship. One had been on the bridge and had been removed before we arrived, probably by the crew when they abandoned ship. The second one had been located in Flight Control. It had also been removed. It took Darin the better part of three hours before he found the third computer system co-located in one of the coffin chambers. It didn't look anything like we thought it should. Initially we thought it was a sub-system dedicated to monitoring the five thousand coffins. It took almost two hours to determine it hadn't been booby-trapped and then we removed it in such a way the data was preserved.

There were five coffin chambers, each with one thousand coffins. As we worked our way forward from the shuttle bay, we examined most of them and came to the conclusion something had gone terribly wrong with the ship. It appeared almost half of the coffins contained the remains of deceased passengers. We came upon a laboratory area we think contained fertilized embryos that were supposed to be held in stasis. About half of them were missing, the remainder looked like they were decayed. We would have to wait until we returned to New Jerusalem to find out exactly.

When our twelve hours were up, we left the coffin ship and began our return to Earth. Our copilot, Jack, conducted a scan of the land below the coffin ship to see if we could locate the ship's passengers and crew who survived. Several sites were promising and would be investigated at a later date.

Hiroshi and I agreed we had an exceptionally successful mission. However, it was just the beginning.

Mission Log Debriefing—Dr. John Sanborn

I had the honor of downloading the mission logs from the coffin ship. The ship was named *Blue Streak.* The log stated the name came from the dark-blue of the ship's hull when the shields were active, and its incredible speed. All of us were amazed they could construct a ship which could reach a quarter of the speed of light. They would have to have accelerated at several Gs and maintained it for perhaps a month or more to reach that speed. According to Dr. Soo Song, a human body couldn't tolerate that level of stress. Senior Healer Johnson suggested the coffins may have had provisions to mitigate the effects of G loading. Marine Captain Doug Fleharty added they could have developed inertia dampeners. For some reason, his suggestion resulted in Commander Koyama and Admiral Lawrence laughing loudly. Since I had no idea what an inertia dampener was, I concluded it was an inside joke.

The outbound leg of their trip encountered difficulties right from the beginning. After several long delays in launching, they arrived at Proxima B approximately twenty-five years after *Hope* began her voyage back to Earth. They lost about five hundred of the passengers and crew due to problems with the coffins and their support equipment. I found their reaction to the loss to be significant. The log stated the amount of loss was anticipated and was considered acceptable. They had similar losses for the fertilized embryos. To me, their acceptance of such losses indicated they were desperate to escape Earth and The Plague. Although not mentioned directly in the logs, there were some references which seemed to imply the workers constructing the *Blue Flash* became infected and there was great concern the passengers and crew would become infected as well.

Their method of dealing with the workers who contacted The Plague appeared brutal. There was supporting material that indicated they were immediately executed, their bodies cremated along with all their possessions and the ashes launched into deep space. By the time the ship was ready to launch The Plague has grown exponentially and chaos prevailed over most of the Earth.

One would expect the ship would have undergone trial runs to ensure everything worked correctly. I could find no mention of any trails being performed. When they left LEO, it was in a panic. Many of the passengers had not been placed in their coffins or connected to their life support equipment. None of the crew had that luxury which should have been standard procedure. The log mentions several crew members succumbed to the initial two G acceleration rate while assisting the passengers.

Blue Streak arrived at Proxima B much later than originally planned. They had major problems with the propulsion system and were only able to manage a maximum speed of twenty percent the speed of light, and sometimes not even that much. It took them a little over twenty years to make the trip.

The surviving passengers and crew went through a two week rehabilitation regimen aboard the ship prior to being shuttled down to the planet's surface. They met with the colonists and attended several briefings over the next month. The colony had made good strides and had grown substantially during their first twenty-five years. Apparently, the leaders of the *Blue Streak* program had comm'd the colony, told them of their plan to visit and asked them what they needed in terms of equipment and supplies. The message took four years to reach the colony. The colony leaders put together a shopping list and sent it back to Earth, which took another four years.

Due to delays, *Blue Streak* arrived twenty-five years after *Hope* had departed. The ship remained in orbit around Proxima B for two years assisting the colonists. Many aboard *Blue Steak* wanted to remain with the colony, they were afraid The Plague would still be active. After the colonist leaders determined how many new people they could support, they decided to accept three thousand of *Blue Streak's* passengers as permanent residents. Approximately fifteen hundred passengers and crew began their trip back to Earth.

The return trip turned into a disaster. From what I could piece together, it appeared they used a lot more of the cryo-sleep nutrient supply then they planned for on their journey to Proxima B. After the crew assisted the returning passengers into their sleep chambers, the captain informed the crew they had only enough nutrient supply for half of them. The leaders of the colony absolutely refused to take any more of the *Blue Streak's* passengers than the three thousand they had agreed to. They claimed they would not have enough rations to feed the colony if they took more. They were already surviving on reduced calorie diets.

The captain informed the crew they all would be saved. He would be the one to decide which passengers would not survive the trip home. Those he chose not to survive would be given painless lethal injections instead of any nutrients.

When the ship returned to Earth, it was automatically placed in a synchronous orbit by the computer over what used to be called Europe. When the crew and passengers were revived, it was discovered only five hundred had survived the journey. The ship's captain was not one of the survivors.

They used the remaining shuttles to transport the survivors to the surface. Half of the shuttles had been left on Proxima B. They also used the shuttles to take whatever they could scavenge from the ship before they abandoned it.

Blue Streak's story was a tragic one. It reminded me of the similar fate of the generation ship *Faith*. The next chapter in the *Blue Streak* story was for us to determine what happened to the survivors.

<u>Who Hacked the Security Bots? — Dr John Sanborn</u>

Once I determined the vids from the two security bots' recordings of The Moses' death were frauds, the next step was to determine how the bots were hacked. I was aware that Commander Hiroshi Koyama felt it was carried out by people from *Blue Steak,* however I had my doubts. I felt confident it had to have been someone who was intimately familiar with how our security bots functioned. That meant I probably knew the hacker.

The bot's designs are a very closely held secrets. Only a few people knew the details of how they worked. Thanks to The Moses promoting me to leader of the Information Technology Group, the hacker most likely worked for me. There were over fifty people in the IT group, five leaders with nine or ten people reporting to each leader. My first task was to determine likely candidates for the hack and then narrow it down to the actual hacker.

The first criteria I looked at were skill levels. Which of my people had the ability to pull off this type of hack? I felt there were only four people out of the fifty plus who could have possibly carried off such a sophisticated operation. It required exceptionally high programming skills. I considered for a moment that perhaps more than one person was involved, but thought it was unlikely: too high a risk of detection.

I felt the actual work must have been done in one of our own labs. We had the most advanced computer systems in all of New Jerusalem and the fraudulent vids were of the highest quality. It could have only been done on one of our systems.

I began checking the activity logs of my four suspects. All of them were busy with high priority projects. I noticed several of the projects with the highest priorities had been to update our security bots' capabilities. Two of my candidates were leading two separate projects. They both required overtime and I noticed there were times when both had come in for evening or night shift coverage. All the overtime work was done just prior to The Moses' death.

It was time to confront the remaining candidates. I wanted Simon to be the interrogator.

The first candidate was one of my team leaders, a woman name Natalie. I called her in for a project review meeting. When she entered the conference room, she was startled to see Simon sitting next to me. "Why is SSP Simon attending this review?" she asked with a quaver in her voice.

"Sit down Natalie," I said sternly. "The SSP has some questions he wants to ask you."

She sat down across the table from us. She looked as if she was on the verge of collapsing as Simon stood up, leaned forward, placed his hands on the table, his face only a few inches from hers. "You already know what I'm going to ask, don't you Natalie?" His voice was low and menacing. Tears began to run down her face, and she began to look away from his eyes which seemed to be boring into her. "Look at me!" he shouted, and she flinched as if he had physically struck her.

Her head snapped up and she whispered hoarsely, "I didn't do it. With God as my witness, I swear I didn't do it. A man approached me, he offered me a large sum of money, but I refused. I told him I would turn him into an SP if he didn't leave me alone. He laughed at me. Then he said if I tried to turn him in, I would never see my little boy alive again."

"Who was he?" Simon asked, his voice soothing now.

"I don't know. He approached me just before the entry way when I arrived for night shift several weeks ago. I've been terrified ever since. Please, you have to believe me."

The meeting ended. Simon had an SP escort her from the conference room to an empty office. The SP stayed with her while we brought in the other suspect.

He was a relatively young man who joined the IT group a little over two years ago. He had risen through the ranks quickly due to his intuitive grasp of the most complicated software. He was currently a project leader on an upgrade for security bots. His name was Alfred and he also looked startled to seen Simon sitting next to me.

"What's he doing here?" he said in a belligerent tone. "Does he have a high enough clearance to hear about my work?"

Without speaking, Simon shot out his hand and grabbed Alfred by the collar, pulled him across the table until their foreheads were touching and yelled into his face, "You are in so much trouble, punk. You're lucky I don't kill you right here, right now." He shoved him backwards so hard Alfred slammed into his chair and almost went over backwards.

Alfred regained his balance and came out of his chair and screamed at Simon, "You can't treat me like that, you big buffoon. You know what you are? You're a joke, a has-been old fart that has outlived his usefulness. It's you that's going to die. You're next on the list. I can't wait to see…"

Simon's fist hit him squarely in the face with such force it broke his nose and knocked out several teeth. Alfred fully went over backwards in his chair hitting the back of his head hard on the tile floor. He lay motionless as I got up and looked at him lying there unconscious. I turned to Simon and said, "I guess we have our man. I hope he survives to tell us who put him up to it."

The New Tribunal Plus One—Paul and John

We were sitting in our Temple office when the invitation arrived. Rear Admiral Lawrence and Governor Stewart requested our presence at the Tribunal office concerning a matter of some importance. We were busy, but we didn't think it wise to say no. We dropped everything and hurried to the Tribunal office on the other side of the Temple.

"Gentlemen, thank you for coming on such short notice," said Governor Stewart as an aide ushered us into the small conference room. "Please help yourselves to pastries and drinks and have a seat."

We thanked him, took small plates with pastries and fruit juices, and sat down at the conference table across from the governor and Rear Admiral Lawrence.

Rear Admiral Lawrence began. "We are in the middle of a crisis and we need your help."

We looked at each other, both of us confused, then back at the two Tribunal members. "How can we help?" asked Paul.

"Senior Judge Aaron has declined our request for him to temporarily take The Moses' place on the Tribunal," answered the admiral. "He feels it would be a conflict of interest. We're not sure what he meant by that, but we need a replacement, someone not part of the *Hope* crew. We'd like the two of you to become members of the Tribunal."

"Why us?" we said simultaneously. "Surely, New Jerusalem has more experienced people than ourselves who could better help you lead…"

The governor raised his hand to silence us and said, "We want someone the people of New Jerusalem trust. The Moses was a dynamic leader, both in religion and government. You have assumed his religious leadership role. We believe the people trust you and respect you, more so than anyone else we can think of. Senior Judge Aaron was added to the Tribunal as a temporary replacement mainly because of his seniority. However, the people fear him, they don't trust him. So, are you willing to accept this additional position?"

We answered simultaneously again, "Of course, how could we refuse such an honor. We hope and pray we can live up to your expectations."

"Excellent!" said the admiral. "Welcome aboard. I have one more question before we get into the main topic of today's meeting. Do you always speak at the same time? I mean, we saw you speak that way in your church services on the Ten Commandments, but that was scripted and rehearsed. Our conversation today wasn't scripted and yet you spoke as one person. Do you always speak in unison?"

"Not always," we said in unison. "What about the name?"

"What do you mean?" asked the admiral.

"When we become members of the Tribunal, we will be four, not three. A tribunal implies three people."

The governor replied, "We thought of that. We are thinking about changing the name to Tribunal Plus One. Each or your votes will count as a half, so we still have an odd number of votes for tie-breaker situations. Of course, this assumes you will both vote the same way on every issue. Do you always agree on things?"

"Almost never," we said at the same time.

They all got refills on the drinks and took the last of the pastries before sitting back down at the conference table. The admiral showed pictures of his son at his recent birthday party. He just turned eleven and was doing well in middle school. He split his spare time between weight training and martial arts.

Not to be upstaged, the governor showed vids of his daughter at the Father-Daughter Dance at her school then followed with her musical recital playing the violin as part of a string quartet.

The two older men asked us how the Ten Commandment training was progressing. We were very enthusiastic about how well it was going. People who were reluctant to accept Christianity but were dedicated believers in the Old Testament were flocking to the classes and were even beginning to see how they wouldn't be giving up their OT beliefs, just expanding them by looking at the New Testament.

There was a lull in the conversation. A few moments passed before there was a knock on the door. The admiral said, "Come in, please." The door opened and in walked Medical Director Dr. Soo Song and SSP Simon. Simon looked over at the credenza and frowned when he noticed the pastry tray was empty. The governor saw his expression and said to the aide standing by the open door, "Could we please get a refill on the pastries. I don't believe our other guests have had time to eat breakfast this morning."

The aide left and returned shortly with a tray stacked high with a wide assortment of pastries including green chili bagels, Simon's favorites. His frown changed immediately to a smile as he filled his plate and poured glasses of orange juice for Soo and himself.

After a few bites of the bagel and a sip of juice, he began. "Thanks to Dr. Sanborn, we now know who created the fake vids of The Moses' death. His name is Alfred and he works for Dr. Sanborn in the IT group. Unfortunately, we aren't sure who ordered Alfred to create the fake vids or their motives for killing our religious leader. However, we have some promising possibilities."

"How did you find out Alfred was the one who created the fake vids?" asked Governor Stewart.

Simon raised his right hand. It was badly swollen with a rainbow of red, yellow and purple colors. "I'm a very persuasive interrogator. He shared with me that he was offered a large sum of money and promised to be promoted to lead the IT department when the New Order took over."

"Wow!" we said in unison. "This sounds like the beginning of a revolution."

"Quite right my friends," replied Simon. "I think it is an attempt to stop Christianity from changing New Jerusalem forever. They've gone underground since many of their leaders were banished from New Jerusalem after the riots. The assassination of The Moses was just the first step, blaming me as the murderer was step two. I expect the attacks to get much worse very shortly."

Rear Admiral Lawrence asked Simon, "Who made the offer to Alfred?"

"At the moment we don't know for sure, but I have my suspicions. Alfred said he was approached by two people, one man and one woman. They wore masks and their voices were altered. I asked Alfred to repeat exactly what they said. He claimed he could repeat the conversation verbatim. Based on what he said, I'm almost certain the man was Senior Judge Aaron and the woman was Chief Senior Healer Johnson."

"Double Wow!!" we said at the same time.

The governor exclaimed, "This just keeps getting better and better."

"Alfred added a couple of further tidbits of information before he was…removed."

Rear Admiral Lawrence spoke up strongly, "Not permanently, I hope."

Simon glanced at his wrist chrono and then said, "Not yet."

"As soon as this meeting is over the members of the Tribunal wish to see him. Do you understand?" Everyone knew that was an order from the admiral.

"Of course, admiral. I'll escort you myself," replied Simon.

Simon took a deep breath then let it out slowly. "Alfred said that The Moses didn't die by an assassin sneaking into his quarters. He showed me the real vids from the security bots. After The Moses went to bed no one entered his room, no one administered the neurotoxin to him while he slept. We would be back to square one if it wasn't for some critical information from Dr. Song."

"First, before the good doctor speaks to us, my last piece of information from Alfred. He said there is an underground of over a hundred members poised to attack the city. He said they call themselves The Zealots for God. Their goal is to execute everyone currently in power; to return to the way it was before *Hope* returned and ruined everything. The last were his words, not mine."

Dr. Song waited a moment to make sure Simon was finished, she then said, "I've been asked to share information with you all regarding Chief Senior Healer Johnson. I've done some extensive research on her medical background as well as her political and religious leanings. CSH Johnson has been a doctor for over thirty years. She moved up the ranks of healer achieving the highest rank possible for her profession. She is now a consulting physician which means she rarely sees patients anymore. Instead, other doctors come to her for advice on how to diagnosis patients or how to conduct a difficult surgery. When she completed medical school, she spent the first five years of her career in medical research. Her area of specialty was poisons, both natural and synthetic. The last two years of her research was limited to synthetic neurotoxins and their vaccines." She paused to let us consider the implications of what she had just said.

"The last year of her research, she was given a specialty award by the board of medical educators for her contributions to understanding synthetic neurotoxins, their creation, their methods of delivery and their vaccines."

She paused again and Simon said, "This is all very interesting, but it would be circumstantial evidence in a court of law. Speaking of the law, please tell everyone about her relationship with Senior Judge Aaron."

Dr. Song nodded her head. "The medical school happened to be located adjacent to the law college. According to records, Judge Aaron was attending the law college when Healer Johnson was doing her toxin research at the medical school. There were unsubstantiated rumors that they were romantically involved for almost five years. However, Judge Aaron was married. His wife was working to put him through law school. Within a year after becoming a judge, Aaron's wife died under mysterious circumstances. Charges were brought against Healer Johnson for murder. However, all evidence was considered circumstantial and she was acquitted of all charges."

The governor asked, "Was Judge Aaron presiding over the trial?"

"No, but he was acting as Healer Johnson's defense counsel," Dr. Song replied. "The SP who filed the initial charges was not satisfied by the verdict and made it a personal vendetta to get the case re-opened. He claimed to find hard evidence and was in the process of filing new charges, when he died of a heart attack. He had no prior history of a heart condition and was only thirty-six years old. Four years after the SP's heart attack, Judge Aaron and Healer Johnson were married. Their marriage lasted seven years and there were no children. That concludes my report," Dr. Song said quietly.

Everyone turned toward Simon in anticipation of his comments. "I have enough evidence to interrogate both of them. With the Tribunal's approval, I will begin immediately. I strongly suggest we initiate martial law as quickly as we can.

Interrogations—SSP Simon

I chose to begin my interrogations with Chief Senior Healer Johnson. I suspected she was the one who supplied the neurotoxin that was used to murder The Moses, but no one could figure out how the poison got into his system. I had one clue that I wanted to explore.

Shortly after our meeting with the new Tribunal, excuse me, the Tribunal Plus One, I had Healer Johnson detained, followed by an official arrest. Of course, she protested. She demanded to know why she was being arrested, but I could see the fear in her eyes when I viewed the vid of her arrest; she knew. That fear came from guilt. I was sure of it.

We kept her in a private detention cell for several hours to let that guilt fester within her. She was then transferred to the interrogation room in shackles. I waited another two hours before entering the room.

She wailed at me when I entered, "Simon, what is the meaning of this? What murder am I being charged with? What…"

I turned on her and shouted in my most terrifying voice, "Silence!!! I will ask the questions here." I stared at her for a moment and then sat down across the table from her. I snapped opened the file I carried in and pretended to be reviewing it. I closed it with a flurry, raised my eyes to glare at her and said in a calmer voice, "You are not being charged with a murder." I paused for a moment to let her hope for freedom build, and then said, "You are being charged with *three* murders." I watched as her hope dissolved and the fear returned. No, not fear, terror.

"You are being charged with the murder of Judge Aaron's wife, the murder of SP Atkins, and, most recently, the murder of The Moses." I could see her terror increasing as I listed off the three murders.

Her eyes grew wider with each charge. When I finished she babbled at me. "No, I was acquitted of the first two. You can't…"

I slammed down my hand on the table and shouted at her, "Silence! We have new evidence, an eyewitness to all three murders, the murders you committed with the synthetic neurotoxin you created. You are going to be stoned to death for your crimes."

She jerked back as if she had been punished by a protector's wand. "Who is the eyewitness?" she asked, her voice barely a whisper.

"Who do you think?" I snarled.

"It could only be one person, Aaron," she answered

"There are a lot of men named Aaron in New Jerusalem."

"There is only one Judge Aaron. He must be the one. After all I have done for him, he betrayed me? I can't believe it. Why would he do that?"

"It was an attempt to try and save himself from the stoning pit. He claimed he tried to stop you, but you were determined…"

"That liar!!!" she screamed. "It was all his plan, not mine. He begged me to get rid of his wife so we could be together. He said we had to kill the SP before he exposed both of us. I never poisoned any of them. I gave him the neurotoxin and he had someone else poison them."

"What about The Moses?" I asked.

"The same way," she answered. "He asked me for a poison that could not be detected and would not become active for at least three hours."

"Did he tell you who the target was?"

"No. He said it would be better if I didn't know. I told him I wouldn't do it; I was done with killing. He said he would tell you about the other two murders if I didn't give him the poisons. So I relented. I was shocked to find out he used the poison on The Moses."

I turned away from the healer toward the vid com and asked, "Are all the comments made by the healer truthful?"

An electronic voice replied instantly, "Yes, SSP. All the healer's comments are the truth as she knows them."

I turned back to the healer and said, "If you continue to help me, there is a chance you will not have to be sent to the stoning pit. Do you agree to help?"

Her head bobbed up and down as she answered, "I'll answer all your questions SSP. I'll do anything to avoid the pit."

I had the protector take her back to her holding cell. I took a few minutes to plan my interrogation of Judge Aaron. I left the interrogation room and spent an hour in my office. I had lunch, answered some com messages and let Judge Aaron stew in his holding cell.

I picked up the folder from my desk and walked to the interrogation room. I stopped at the command center and spoke with the protector monitoring the room vid. "How's he doing?" I asked.

"He's not happy, but that's to be expected. He's been shouting a lot, so I turned off the sound," answered the protector.

I nodded and said, "Turn it back on. I'm going in."

I opened the door and walked in without looking at the judge. He began shouting at me, that I was breaking the law by imprisoning him without charges, that he was going to have my badge, and so on and so forth. I sat down and placed the file on the desk before finally looking up at him. "Please sit down, judge," I said calmly, almost cheerfully.

He stopped shouting and said, "Release me at once. You have no legal right to imprison me."

I opened the file and said, "You are being charged with two counts of accessory to murder and one count of murder. There are pending charges for inciting a riot, treason and sedition. Are you happy now?"

He began to bluster, almost incoherently. I ignored him. When he paused for a breath, I said. "Please sit down, judge."

"Senior Judge," he shouted at me as he finally took a seat. "I'm to be addressed as Senior Judge Aaron."

I shook my head and smiled as I answered, "Not for long."

"You dare threaten me?!!"

I jumped up and shouted back at him, "Shut up and sit down. From this moment on you will only speak to answer my questions."

He also jumped up and screamed, "You have no authority over me. I will speak when I choose."

I reached behind me and pulled out a protector's wand from my belt. Before he realized what I was doing, I leaned across the table and stunned him on the shoulder. It was only a level one stun, but he dropped into his chair, his eyes wide with fear.

"We have two witnesses who have testified against you on these charges. You are responsible for the murder of your wife and for the murder of SP Adkins. You paid someone to take a neurotoxin and use it to kill them both. In addition, you are personally responsible for the recent death of our leader, The Moses. The assassination of The Moses is considered more heinous than murder. The penalty when convicted is death by stoning. And as sure as I sit here you *will* be convicted."

He glared at me, I could see I hadn't broken him yet. I was sure it was only a matter of time. A slight smile formed on his face, just a trace as he said, "Do you know what will happen if I'm convicted?"

"Of course, I know. You will die."

He continued to smile and said, "Yes, I will die as a martyr for the cause, and hundreds, perhaps thousands, of those who share my beliefs will rise up and smite the Christian devils who have destroyed our way of life. The leaders of *Hope* will go first, then the traitors from New Jerusalem. Finally, we will drive out the demons from the Temple and rededicate it to the old ways of worship."

He had a maniacal expression on his face as he continued his rant. "You won't be able to stop us. It will be like a tidal wave of truth flowing over the Christian lies. You won't be able to stop us," he said once more and then began to laugh.

I waited for his laughter to stop before I said, "Yuk it up judge." I turned to the vid cam and said, "Protector, please show vid A7."

It showed hundreds of men and woman being rounded up by *Hope* marines and New Jerusalem protectors. They were escorted outside the Outer Wall to the dormitories that had been converted to temporary jail cells.

I watched the judge as his confidence began to drain from him. I added my narration. "Ever since we interrogated Alfred, we've been operating under martial law. We quietly began detaining those suspected of being part of your gang of misfits. Most of them readily identified other members in order to lessen the penalty for their own crimes. Alfred also gave us leads as to where caches of weapons and explosives were kept. After interrogating some of our suspects we believe we have found all of the caches. So I think your revolution is going to die along with you, *judge.*"

I turned around just in time to see the judge leaping across the table going for my throat. I had my wand in hand and drove it into his stomach before his cuffed hands could reach me. I stunned him twice at a level five setting and watched him crumble to the floor in pain. He lost consciousness a moment later. I said, "I hope that really hurt." I couldn't think of anything else to say.

The Trials—Tribunal /Rear Admiral Lawrence

I was chosen to be the spokesman for the Tribunal Plus One. Three citizens of New Jerusalem were on trial; Alfred White, IT, charged with accessory to murder; Chief Senior Healer Martha Johnson, charged with accessory to murder; and Senior Judge Walter Aaron, charged with murder, treason and sedition. Each of the three was tried separately.

The first two were tried before the Tribunal, the last before a jury of twelve men and women from New Jerusalem and the surrounding suburbs. For security reasons, no spectators were permitted in the courtroom. However, each trial was made available for viewing over vid coms. Legal counsel was provided to the Tribunal by three judges

First up on the docket was Alfred White. He pled guilty to the charges. Because of his assistance in providing valuable information regarding the other two plaintiffs, his sentence was limited to two years of probation living in the dormitories outside the Outer Wall. Any violation of the rules of his probation would result in him being banished for life from the city.

Next up was Chief Senior Healer Martha Johnson. She worked out a plea agreement and her charges were reduced to first degree manslaughter. She pled guilty to this charge. She was removed from her position as leader of the New Jerusalem medical community. Her title was changed to Healer. She was not allowed to operate or partake in any research without explicit written permission of the Tribunal. She was limited to teaching at the medical school while she was on a five year probation period. She also had to reside in the dormitory outside the Outer Wall and any violation of her probation would result in her banishment for life from the city.

There were many who felt this sentence wasn't severe enough. Several high ranking citizens thought she should have been executed.

Fortunately for the healer, they were not willing to challenge the verdict.

Senior Judge Walter Aaron was the last to be tried. His plea was not guilty by reason of justifiable homicide. No member of the Tribunal had ever heard of that plea, but apparently it was one of New Jerusalem's many laws.

The jury was sworn in and the trial began. He served as his own counsel. In his opening remarks he said The Moses had been a great religious leader as well as the leader of New Jerusalem's government. It was unfortunate that he was seduced by the people of *Hope*. The New Testament was a lie which led to many sacrilegious changes. If The Moses was not stopped, the city would be in ruins. The only way for order to be restored was to begin with the death of The Moses followed by the death or expulsion of the *Hope* people forever from the city.

He testified The Moses' death was painless. "He died peacefully in his sleep. I pray that God will forgive him for his blasphemies."

It went on and on like that. It seemed it would never end. Eventually, he stopped. He turned to the jury and gave his final summation, "Surely, you must see the necessity for The Moses' death. Therefore, you must acquit me on the grounds of justifiable murder."

Simon stood and addressed the members of the Tribunal. "Would you permit me one question of the defendant?" We all nodded in agreement. He turned towards Judge Aaron and asked, "Could you please tell the court how the neurotoxin ended up in the Moses' body?"

He seemed surprised by the question. "Of course," he said. "It was coated on a paper he was reading just before he had his dinner. When he touched the paper, the toxin was absorbed through the pores of his fingers. The toxin molecules were coated by a layer of fat. It took approximately three hours for the fat to dissolve in his blood. He was asleep by then. Once the fat was dissolved the toxin became active. At that point it took about five minutes for him to succumb. The paper used as the carrier for the neurotoxin had an undercoating of a chemical that vaporized the remaining toxin within five to six hours. By morning all trace of the poison was gone. It was really just simple chemistry."

The jury filed into a room adjacent to the court to determine a verdict. Ten minutes later, they filed out and handed me a note. I read it aloud. "We the jury find the defendant guilty of murder in the first degree. We recommend death by stoning as quickly as possible."

I excused the jury, then turned to Judge Aaron and said, "You've been found guilty by a jury of your peers and you…"

"They were not my peers," he said calmly. You were sure to stack the jury with Christians. No one truly represented my position."

"That's not true, Aaron," I answered, purposely dropping the title. He was no longer a judge. "Four of the jurors were Christian, four continued to follow only the Old Testament, the final four had no religious beliefs at all. All twelve of them voted for you to be stoned to death for your murder of The Moses."

He didn't seem too surprised by my comments. He just shrugged his shoulders and said, "So be it."

An hour later he was taken to the stoning pit, his hands shackled to a low post to keep him in the center of the pit. The paved walkway around the pit was jammed with the residents from New Jerusalem. Some of them were angry, others crying, all of them holding a stone in their hand. Simon stood directly in front of Aaron and shouted to be heard over the crowd noise. "Quiet please. Just a moment of quiet." When the noise subsided, Simon asked, "Do you have any last words? Keep it brief."

Aaron looked briefly at all the people waiting to take his life and smiled. In a loud voice he said, "You think this is the end? You think the killing has ended? You fools, this is only the beginning. Wait till you see the *Blue Streak*. They will destroy the Temple and kill you all. Kill you all," he repeated and began laughing maniacally.

Simon stepped forward and threw a large rock very fast which struck Aaron in the head. In less than a minute his corpse was covered by rocks.

Blue Streak Threat—Commander Hiroshi Koyama

In light of Aaron's last words, the investigation for *Blue Streak* survivors was ratcheted up to the highest priority. We resumed our efforts with renewed enthusiasm. It was decided we would approach our activities from multiple directions. Most, but not all, were centered on what we knew regarding *Blue Streak.*

It was suggested by Doug, newly promoted Marine Major Doug Fleharty, we consider tracking the people that had been banished from New Jerusalem. He thought some of them were military conscripts who had fought against us in the last war. With their military training they could be a threat, especially if the remnants of the *Blue Streak* crew got to them. It was a good idea. I put him in charge of following up on it.

Several years ago we came upon a *Blue Streak* shuttle close to New Jerusalem attempting to make off with a nuclear bomb. We spent several months attempting to hunt them down without any success. I decided to do another limited search of the area around the city. Shuttle Sierra was getting reconfigured for our search of possible European sites we'd discovered during our return from the mothership. During the week it took to upgrade Sierra, I assigned Trish and Jack to pilot two smaller shuttles to do fast surveys within a hundred mile radius of New Jerusalem for any potential threats. They left immediately, each with a crew of three techs plus one marine.

By the end of the week they completed their search. They found no obvious threats. They spent a couple of days debriefing the rest of my team and decompressing from their stressful mission. By the time the Sierra was ready, so were they.

At Rear Admiral Lawrence's request, Commander White was reinstated to active duty to oversee all military operations. The admiral told me, "He grumbled a bit, but I could tell he was glad to be back on duty. He turned the recreation activities over to someone he referred to as a 'muscle bound, wannabe civilian who idolizes me.' It was good to see he was still the same modest man we have grown to love."

We lifted off for Europe with a crew of eight. We had two marines for security. All of us were well armed and Sierra retained all her weaponry from our search for the mothership.

Trish selected a sub-orbital flight to save on reaction mass. It also gave us the shortest time to contact with our first possible intruder camp. The three G launch didn't seem so bad. I guess we were adapting to the G loads.

We accelerated to just short of orbital velocity, cut our engines, nosed over and then began the long weightless glide to our first target. The engines were restarted to slow our decent and then to maintain a thirty thousand foot fly-by of the target.

"Tally ho," shouted Joker. "Two clicks east of the river. Sensors count two hundred people: men, women and children. Lots of domestic animals. No shuttles, Nothing mechanical. I think they're locals, not *Blue Streak* crew."

We moved on to the next site with the same results. As we began our flight to the third site, one of the techs said, "I have long range contact with a much larger town. No shuttles but many vehicles, from small to large. Estimate of population from the size of the town would be approximately five hundred, however, none are detected. A large hanger-like building east of…"

Joker interrupted excitedly, "I have contact at eighty thousand feet and climbing, heading west."

"Is it a shuttle?" I asked feeling my own emotions rising.

"No sir," answered Joker. "It's *five* shuttles in tight formation!"

My stomach clenched as I replied, "Can you tell where they're headed?"

There was a brief pause. "If they maintain present course and speed they will be over New Jerusalem in five hours!"

Now my heart began to really beat faster. "Trish, plot a course…"

"Aye sir, already done. Sit down and strap in. We need to pull some serious Gs to beat them to our city."

"Joker," I yelled as Trish began a climbing turn and shoved the throttles to max. It felt like an elephant just sat down on my chest, a very large elephant. I manage to squeeze out my question. "Do they see us?"

After what sounded like a painful groan, Joker answered, "No sir. Not yet."

I focused on trying to breathe and hoped everyone else was too. "Trish, how many Gs? How long?"

It took her a long time to answer. In a strained voice she answered, "Approaching eight Gs. An hour, maybe longer."

I sent a quick transmission to Commander White warning him of the potential attack. Almost immediately, I received a response. "Message received. We'll be ready. Out."

I could feel consciousness slipping away. My last thought before the inevitable happened was, *Where are the damned inertia dampeners when you need them?*

Part 3

Another Armageddon?

10 Years Later

<u>Beginning A Decade—Rear Admiral David Lawrence</u>

The last decade ended in panic for the good citizens of New Jerusalem. We thought we had ended the insurrection and the planned violence. There was almost a collective sigh of relief signaling closure. However, as Senior Judge Aaron, the instigator of the violence, the orchestrator of the assassination of our beloved Moses, stood in the stoning pit to await his death all that changed.

He said New Jerusalem was doomed to destruction from an outside force. Remnants from the crew of *Blue Steak,* an interstellar ship from Europe, would attack the city soon. All would be destroyed.

I think most of us thought that was just the bluster of a soon-to-be-executed man. I was one of them … until we got the com from Hiroshi less than an hour later. Five very advanced shuttles were on their way from Europe. Our shuttle, Sierra, had given chase, it was doubtful they would be able to intercept them.

Commander Henry White had been brought out of retirement to handle such an emergency. He never missed a beat in making sure all of New Jerusalem's defenses were in place and active. All of our shuttles from *Hope* were sent out to intercept the enemy an hour from New Jerusalem.

Everything we needed to repel the attackers was ready. Every military trained man and woman was on high-alert, the civilians had been moved to the shelters in the ancient's lab.

It turned out it was all for nothing. The *Blue Streak* shuttles were not coming to attack. They were coming to seek asylum. When our shuttles scanned them, no weapons were detected.

There were some among us who thought we should destroy them. Maybe it was a trap of some type, or maybe not, but one of their shuttles *had* fired on Sierra several years ago. We needed to be careful … and we were.

The five European shuttles touched down a mile from the gates of the city. After a rigorous search of every passenger, they were placed onboard large people carriers and ferried to the main gate. They remained under guard by *Hope's* marines and the city's protectors as they walked to the Temple. A quick headcount determined there were almost five hundred people. They were broken up into groups of no more than fifty and dispersed around the cavernous Sanctuary.

A group of ten men and women came forward, describing themselves as the Ruling Council. They were escorted to a large conference room to meet with our Tribunal Plus One and other high ranking city officials to determine exactly why they were here. Before we called the meeting to order, we invited them to join us in some refreshments and the opportunity to use the restrooms.

We went through the formalities of introductions first, after which I made some brief opening comments. "We welcome you to the city of New Jerusalem. I have to admit, your arrival took us somewhat by surprise. Please forgive the military presence; we thought you were going to attack us. We'd like to extend to you our hospitality, however, before we can do that we need to get some information. Be advised, we have knowledge about *Blue Streak* and its mission to Proxima B. What we are primarily interested in is what happened after you returned to Earth."

A tall blond man with blue eyes stood and said, "I am Klaus and the lady sitting beside me is my wife Marta." He gestured to his left at an attractive middle aged woman, also with blond hair and blue eyes. "Our Ruling Council has asked me to speak on their behalf. First let me thank you for not shooting us down when we arrived in your airspace." He paused for a moment and smiled as several people from the city chuckled at his comment. "Our lead shuttle was having difficulties connecting with your com system."

His expression became serious as he continued, "We left our base camp in Europe to escape certain annihilation. After spending two years searching, we finally discovered the perfect place to live. We built permanent structures, planted crops in the most fertile lands you could ask for and gathered livestock into herds on amazing pasture land. It was everything we could have asked for and more. There were other, smaller settlements within a day's walk. The people were friendly and helpful. They helped us get started and we traded with them on a routine basis.

"During our ten years at the site our colony grew and prospered. We hardly ever used our shuttles, we didn't need to fly very often and we were concerned about using up the propulsion system expendables. We were content to..."

Hiroshi stood and interrupted. "Excuse me, Klaus. We were attacked by one of your shuttles several years ago. They were attempting to recover a missing nuclear bomb about fifty miles from New Jerusalem. When we challenged them to identify themselves, they escaped at a very high rate of speed and fired at us with a laser cannon. The blast penetrated our shields and punched a hole in our shuttle's hull."

Klaus looked dumbfounded. He turned to look at the other members of the Ruling Council for a possible explanation. There were rapid conversations in German, at least I think it was German, before he turned back to Hiroshi. "This is the first time I have heard of this incident. Were any of your shuttle crew injured?"

Hiroshi shook his head and then answered, "No, no one was injured, the actual damage was minor and easily repaired. What I want to know is, why did your shuttle fired at us? All we did was to ask your shuttle to identify itself."

In a firm voice Klaus said, "That wasn't our shuttle that fired on you. None of our shuttles are equipped with laser cannons. They were only used as transports. Please, inspect all five of our shuttles before we continue. I want you to see we couldn't have been the ones who fired on you."

Hiroshi comm'd Commander White and had all five of the shuttles inspected. Thirty minutes later the commander comm'd him back. There were no laser cannons on board any of their shuttles. It looked like there had never been any type of weapons installed.

Hiroshi turned back to Klaus and said, "It looks like I owe you an apology. But if it wasn't one of your shuttles who fired on us? Whose was it?"

Klaus' face wore a grim expression as he answered, "I believe the shuttle that attacked you was part of the military forces who forced us to leave our home in Europe."

I stood up abruptly and asked, "Another military presence?! Where did this one come from?"

"I will tell you what I know, admiral. Then I will tell you what we suspect," answered Klaus. "While *Blue Streak* was being built in orbit we were hearing reports, rumors actually, of another MHD powered ship being built. It was being funded by a consortium of Asian countries, mainly China, Japan and Korea. It was supposed to be vastly superior to *Blue Streak* with several major differences. It was also built in orbit, however it was completely built by robots. There were no humans involved in any aspect of its construction. Also the ship had no crew. Again, it was completely controlled by computers equipped with artificial intelligence and it used bots to handle mobile tasks. The cryo-sleep chambers were launched into space preloaded with humans and installed in their respective ports as were the fertilized embryos. I'm not sure when the ship launched, however I know it was well after *Blue Streak* left orbit. One other thing, I can't confirm this either, but I believe the shuttles were also operated by AI computers, completely autonomous from human control. They were also weaponized."

I heard Hiroshi quietly say to Doug with a terrible Spanish accent, "We don't need no stinking inertia dampeners. No people, no problemo."

"Do you know the name of the ship?" I asked Klaus.

"I believe it was called *Golden Dragon*."

<u>Immigrants—Miriam Lawrence & Anna Koyama</u>

The immigrants from *Blue Streak* were phased in with the local immigrants. The Tribunal voted to limit their probationary status to six months instead of the two years for the locals. They were still required to follow all laws and special regulations and faced banishment if they accumulated too many violations.

They were housed together in one of the vacant dormitories. Anna volunteered to hold what she called Get to Know New Jerusalem classes. I handled integrating the people with specific job skills or knowledge into related opportunities. The individuals with military backgrounds were assigned to our respective husbands.

My husband, I now refer to him as *my admiral* since his promotion, headed up a committee to pick the brains of the *Blue Streak* people who had any information about *Golden Dragon*. Commander White, who was still on active duty, organized breakout groups that dealt with such topics as listed below:

- How did the *Blue Streak* people know about New Jerusalem?
- How and when had the *Golden Dragon* attacked them?
- Were there any human beings left on *Golden Dragon* or just bots?
- What type of weapons did they have?
- Did *Golden Dragon* know about New Jerusalem?

As you can imagine, all those meetings took up a lot of time. Anna, bless her heart, stepped in and made sure the small children weren't neglected. She and some other mothers volunteered to expand the daycare facilities to accommodate the little ones. Our Dr. Soo Song made sure each child was given a very comprehensive medical exam. Any children with injuries or illnesses was given special treatment.

Anna had the older children enroll in school. She made a point of mixing the children from *Blue Streak* with the New Jerusalem children. She wanted to make sure everyone got to know each other. Ever since she earned her degree in teaching, she and her two older children have made it their business that every child in New Jerusalem got the education they needed. That included children of all the immigrant families.

We talked with many of the *Blue Streak* immigrants about how they were dealing with leaving their homes. Most of them told us they were very sad about leaving. They had worked hard to turn it into a wonderful place to live. After all the turmoil of the trip to Proxima B and back and bouncing around Europe looking for a good place to settle down, they thought they had finally discovered a place where they could put down roots. One family we spoke with said they had finally stopped having nightmares. They felt all the bad times were behind them. And then the creature from *Golden Dragon* arrived and it brought the nightmares back.

We couldn't get any more details from them regarding the creature from *Golden Dragon*, what it said or did, or even what it looked like. It was as if the creature would curse them if they revealed anything about it. We found that very strange. Most of them had been raised Lutheran, the first building they constructed when they founded their home was a church. It was filled to capacity for worship every Sunday. How could believers be so frightened of this creature? Of course we shared this information with our husbands. They said they planned to cover those same questions with the leaders. That information was critical to planning how to defend ourselves from an attack.

Golden Dragon–Klaus & The Ruling Council

Rear Admiral Lawrence gave us the meeting agenda a day in advance. He asked we discuss it amongst ourselves. He stressed they felt it very important to get as much information as we could offer to prepare for a likely attack, no detail was too small or to be considered unimportant.

We spent most of the day putting together our presentation. We all felt our lives, as well as the lives of the people from New Jerusalem, were at stake. If we couldn't defeat them here, there was no hope any of us would survive.

The next morning we all met again at the main conference room in the Temple. The night before, we prepared our best clothes to wear to the meeting. We noticed at our first meeting the military people all wore their uniforms and the civilian leaders wore suits. We *Blue Streak* people were still wearing our travel clothes which made us feel very uncomfortable. Most of us came from German ancestry and it was impressed on us to dress appropriately for important occasions. At the time, I couldn't think of anything more important than this meeting.

After everyone entered the conference room, the admiral nodded for me to begin. I stood and moved to the rostrum set up at the head of the table. We thought of ourselves as a religious people, always beginning important meetings with a prayer. My first words were, "I would like to begin this meeting with a prayer. Could we all stand and bow our heads please?" As everyone stood I saw Chaplain George's face light up and he nodded his agreement. "Our heavenly father, our all powerful creator and sustainer, we come to you this morning with heavy hearts. We fear an enemy, a strong and resourceful enemy, wants to destroy us. We meet today to discuss ways to defeat this enemy, we ask for your guidance and inspiration.

We know all things are possible for you and we ask for your blessing. We ask these things in the name of your son, Jesus Christ. Amen."

There was a resounding Amen from all those present. I felt comforted by the strength of their voices. I raised my head and said, "Thank you. Please be seated.

"This morning we will share with you all that we know of this *Golden Dragon.* The Ruling Council met for most of yesterday to organize our thoughts. We also brought in others who had some form of contact or at least observed something, anything, regarding these creatures. We encourage interruptions, especially to clarify points that perhaps we glossed over. I also encourage interruptions by my own people if a new piece of information occurs to you.

"Let me begin. Our first observance of a *Golden Dragon* shuttle occurred over several years ago. It was noticed by a few people working outside on a building project. One of the workers was a shuttle pilot. He quickly recognized it was not one of ours nor did he know where it originated. He suggested to the Council that we should set up non-intrusive scanners in case they flew over our position again. Three days later a similar shuttle, perhaps the same one, flew over us at a very high altitude going the opposite direction, perhaps returning from a mission. The scanners captured it and we began an extensive evaluation. We brought two of our computers from the mothership after we abandoned her. They were set up in an IT office and were operational. We fed the scanner data into the computer and asked it to identify the shuttle, if possible. After a few minutes the computer had an answer. There was a high probability, a ninety percent match, with images of a shuttle from the Asian mothership *Golden Dragon.* The information our computer used was dated before that mothership finished construction, changes could have been made before the ship left Earth orbit.

"Besides the information regarding the shuttle, the computer had a great deal of speculative data on the mothership. We have downloaded this information to your computer for further analysis. That took place with the permission of your IT leader, Dr. John Sanborn. Anyone who would like access to that information can contact Dr. Sanborn.

"I would like to give you a brief overview of the distinctive features of *Golden Dragon*. It was a little smaller than *Blue Streak*, and contained cryo-sleep chambers for three thousand passengers. All the passengers were to leave the ship and remain with the Proxima B colony. The ship had no crew. It didn't need one. The ship was designed to be under the total control of an exceptionally sophisticated AI driven computer system. It was a triple redundant system just like *Blue Streak* had. The ship was intended to remain at Proxima B ostensibly to provide security for the colony. We have no idea why it returned to Earth.

"From the data it appears the mothership was also built as a warship. It was supposed to have several types of weapons, including nuclear weapons. At least that's what the initial designs called for. The shuttles were also armed. It is not clear why they felt they needed to arm them.

"After the two shuttle fly overs, it was several months before we saw another shuttle. The first fly over was several miles north of us and we hoped and prayed it had not noticed us. It was the same with the return flight except this time it was several miles to the south. Several weeks went by and we were hopeful we hadn't been noticed, or at least were not considered a threat. Unfortunately it did return and this time the flight path was directly overhead. It made several passes from different vectors. It seemed to get lower with each pass. Our sensors indicated they were scanning our village and surrounding countryside.

"On the last pass, the shuttle was only a few hundred feet above the ground. It stopped and hovered over the village square for a few minutes. It made no sound at all. Everyone was terrified by now. We felt sure we were doomed. Suddenly, the shuttle moved upwards as if it had a chain connected to its back pulling it skyward at an ever increasing speed. In a few minutes it was almost out of sight. When it was just a speck in the blue sky, It began to accelerate eastward. In less than a minute it passed through the sound barrier producing a loud boom, and then continued to increase in speed until it disappeared from view.

"Everyone had been frozen watching the shuttle and wondering if this would be the end of us. The weapons on the shuttle were very visible as it hovered above us. When it left there was a sense of relief, but we realized it was only a matter of time before it would be back. This had only been a recon mission. When they returned, it would be the real thing. We began packing immediately. We had to decide which things we couldn't live without and which we would have to abandon. We were limited to how much space the five shuttles would permit us to take. We quickly discovered many things we thought we couldn't live without had to be discarded. It was painful for all of us."

As I paused for a sip of water, Commander Koyama raised his hand, "Yes, Commander? You have a comment?" I asked.

The commander stood and replied, "How did you know about New Jerusalem. How did you know where to find us?"

As he sat back down, I turned to my wife, Marta, and gestured for her to answer the commander's question. She was dressed in a blue dress that I found very attractive, wearing a string of pearls around her neck and moderately high-heel shoes. I still found her a beautiful woman. However, it was her intelligence I needed right now.

She spoke with confidence. We had anticipated this question and she was prepared to answer. "The databases on our ship's computers made references to the locations where generation ships were built. The closest one to our home was Oak Ridge. We knew the lab location was the place the ship was supposed to return to. Of course we had no assurance the generation ship ever returned from its mission. If it had turned out Oak Ridge was abandoned we considered moving on to the next lab site. However, we knew we wouldn't have enough reaction mass for all the shuttles to go beyond Oak Ridge.

"We attempted to contact you when we crossed the ocean and were back over land. Unfortunately, it appears our long range coms are not compatible with yours. We knew it was a risk to approach you unannounced, but we had no choice."

She nodded to the commander and took her seat. I stood back up and said. "It took us less than a week to get the shuttles packed and ready to leave. We deployed long range sensors in the hope of detecting incoming shuttles from *Golden Dragon*. We practiced and practiced boarding the shuttles as quickly as we could. We didn't want to leave our home until it was absolutely necessary.

"Several months went by without any visits from *Golden Dragon* shuttles. It was as if they had been wiped from the face of the Earth. If that were only the case. One Sunday afternoon after church service, we were holding a church social, a picnic in the park next to the church. It was really more like a potluck feast. Everybody contributed various types of food, including desserts. I was an Elder of the church and Marta and I were mingling with the crowd, wishing everyone a happy afternoon. The church's orchestra began playing a lively polka from the bandstand as the sun went down. People were getting up to dance. I thought this was a splendid idea. We had been living in fear for our lives for so long we needed something to revive us, to give us a few hours to enjoy life like we used to.

"After the first dance, Marta and I stood on the sidelines and watched our friends as they frolicked to the music. Marta pulled on my arm and whispered into my ear, 'Who's the young woman standing next to Joseph? I don't recognize her.' I didn't recognize her either. I thought that was strange since I was pretty sure I knew all of our people. When we approached her, I noticed she looked Asian. I knew we had no one in our group with Asian ancestry. I assumed she was from one of the smaller villages not too far from our town. I spoke to Joseph and said, 'Joseph, could you introduce us to your friend?' When he turned toward us, he looked puzzled. 'What friend, Elder.' I gestured at the young lady standing beside him. He looked around and I could tell he couldn't see her. I turned to the young woman, with fear beginning to grow inside me. I noticed Marta had slipped behind me using my body as a shield in case anything went wrong.

"The woman looked at me with an expressionless face and said, 'He can't see me, Elder. In a few minutes everyone will see me and know who I am.' Her voice had an electronic tone to it, but her German was perfect. She turned and walked through the dancers to the center of the bandstand just as the orchestra finished the second polka. As she made her way to the bandstand, I noticed she walked in a straight line, literally walking through the dancers like a ghost. She turned and faced the dancers and in a loud, high pitched voice she yelled, 'LOOK AT ME!' Suddenly, everyone could see her. She looked around the dance floor from one side to the other. As she did, it seemed as if she was growing larger. She yelled again, this time in a deeper voice, 'WATCH ME AND SEE MY POWER!'

"She began to change. I was aware my fear, my terror, was growing. She slowly morphed from a young, attractive woman into something beastly. As it grew larger, the bandstand began to splinter under the stress of the monster growing inside it. The orchestra members ran screaming from the platform as the beast continued to grow. White smoke began to pour from orifices along the sides of the beast, covering it in a shroud that hid it from view as it continued to morph.

"Suddenly, there was a blinding flash of lightening followed by a deafening roar of rolling thunder which caused the smoke to vanish. There before us was a three stories tall dragon!! Its head was the size of a building and it swung it back and forth taking in the sight of the terrified people from our town. Its eyes were a bright flaming red that seemed to burn right through our flesh when it gazed upon us. The scales that covered its body looked like polished gold. It threw back its head, opened its gigantic mouth and roared fire into the night sky. The roar was so loud the ground shook like an earthquake. The flames had the smell of fire and brimstone. Then it spoke in the deepest bass voice I have ever heard. **'I AM THE GOLDEN DRAGON. I AM YOUR NEW GOD. FROM NOW ON, YOU WILL WORSHIP ONLY ME.'**

"From the steps of the church, our pastor shouted back, 'No we won't. You are the spawn of Satan. We will not worship you. Be gone from us now.' My first thoughts upon hearing the pastor's words were, *Where does he get the courage to stand up against the dragon?* The dragon slowly turned toward the pastor, leaned down until its head was only a few feet from his face. The pastor didn't back down, instead he glared at the dragon in open defiance. The dragon opened his mouth and roared fire upon the pastor and the church consuming everything it touched. All that was left were smoldering ashes. There was much screaming and crying from our people. We were helpless before this cursed monster. The dragon rose up and said to us in his deep, menacing voice, **'IN ONE WEEK, SEVEN DAYS, MY MINIONS WILL ARRIVE AT YOUR TOWN. YOU WILL FOLLOW THEIR**

INSTRUCTIONS. IF YOU DO NOT, I WILL BURN ALL OF YOU TO ASHES AS I BURNED YOUR HOLY MAN.'

"Those were its final words. It crouched on the bandstand and then launched itself into the air, uncoiling massive wings. It was illuminated for a short while by the moon, then quickly disappeared.

"We held a short funeral service for our pastor, then as quickly as we could, we loaded up the shuttles and left our homes, hoping and praying we would find someone to help us. This concludes our comments. Hopefully, we've answered your questions about *Golden Dragon*. All of us pray we can find a way to destroy the dragon and go back to living quiet, peaceful lives."

Commander Koyama raised his hand again. "Yes, Commander? You have a question?" I asked.

"Yes Klaus. Can you tell us if you have any vid data of the appearance of this beast?"

I turned to look at one of the Ruling Council members who nodded his head. I turned back to the commander and said, "Yes we do. We recorded it all."

The commander began to smile and said, "We'd like to take a look at it if we may."

Analysis of the Dragon Vid—Dr. John Sanborn

I wasn't present at the *Blue Steak* briefing. However, as soon as it ended, Hiroshi burst into my office with a data cube. He gave me a quick overview of the meeting as he thrust the data cube into my hand. "That dragon was an avatar, just like the one you created of The Moses when the Angel of Death confronted him in the Sanctuary. It may have been more advanced than the one you created. The fire from the dragon's mouth was real, not sure how they accomplished that. Can you check it out and see if I'm right?"

"Sure," I said. "Let me check my schedule." I pretended to look at my list of appointments and work assignments. "I can get to it sometime next week."

Hiroshi's mouth dropped open, "NO!" he shouted, "Not next week, now, it has to be now. Don't you realize…"

He stopped talking as I began to laugh. Hiroshi began to laugh too. "I think I gotcha. I assume this has the highest priority?"

"Absolutely," he replied as he stopped laughing. "Don't ever do that again." His right hand snaked out so fast I had no time to react.

He slapped me on the shoulder, just a love tap, but it really stung. I made a mental note, *Don't ever mess with Hiroshi over something he considers serious.*

He turned to go. "Please let me know as soon as you finish," he said as he left my office.

I took the cube, inserted it into my computer and went to work. I watched it all the way from the image of the girl walking towards the bandstand until the gold dragon flew off. I replayed it many times applying various filters until I found what I was looking for. Floating inside the image was a material object about the size of a watermelon. Apparently it had stealth shielding. It took three different filters before I was sure it was used to generate the images of the girl and the morphing into the dragon. The smoke and the dragon's fire came from the watermelon.

Further study gave me more detail of its functions. I determined it was controlled by a force similar to our beam; the watermelon had no propulsion system of its own. That led to the question of where the beam came from. It took me more than an hour to discover displacements indicating the shuttle hovering above the *Blue Streak* village. It was operating in a very strong stealth field. It took even more filters to eventually reveal its presence.

I felt I had solved the assignment Hiroshi gave me. However, it generated an even more important question: why would the inhabitants of the shuttle go to such extremes to generate this elaborate deception? If they wanted to capture the village there had to be easier methods.

Fortunately for me, that question was above my pay grade. I comm'd Hiroshi and told him of my results.

Analysis—Commander Hiroshi Koyama

After receiving the results of Dr Sanborn's findings, I immediately scheduled a meeting to brief every one of his results and to discuss possible strategies moving forward. I invited the Tribunal Plus One, now referred to as the Tribunal for the sake of brevity, Dr. Sanborn, SSP Simon and the Ruling Council from *Blue Streak.* We met again in the Temple's large conference room.

Dr. Sanborn was our first speaker. He presented his findings and displayed a vid showing the scene with the young woman and her morphing from a human to the gold dragon. It included the incineration of the pastor and the church. I noticed that many of the Ruling Council declined to watch the horrible scene. Once was enough. Dr. Sanborn then showed the same vid with the appropriate filters revealing only the watermelon-sized source of the avatars. It showed the smoke coming from ports in its outer surface and the nozzle used to shoot out the flames. Speakers were also noted on the watermelon's sides.

He followed this up with the vid using different filters revealing the tractor beam used to move the watermelon into the desired positions and followed the beam upward showing the *Golden Dragon* shuttle.

Klaus stood up, his face was red with rage as he shook his fist at the vid screen. "It was a hoax! Nothing but a hoax! What fools we were. We were driven from our homes by a cursed watermelon!"

As Klaus fell back in his chair, hiding his head in his hands, I said to him and the other Ruling Council members, "It was a very good hoax, Klaus. It would have fooled anyone, us included. In fact, we were fooled initially by a similar hoax almost a decade ago. The question we now need to answer is: Why did they go to all the trouble of creating the hoax? That will be the first order of business after we take a short break."

When we returned, I turned to the vid screen and said, "Print out the following text: Why did *Golden Dragon* create the hoax on the *Blue Streak* village?"

I turned back to the people in the conference room and said, "This is where we offer suggestions to answer that question." I pointed to the printout on the vid screen. "This is called brain storming. All answers will be recorded no matter how frivolous you think they may be. Once we run out of ideas, we will discuss each suggestion and rank them in order of likelihood. Who wants to offer the first suggestion?"

Klaus said in an angry voice, "To capture our village without having to fight for it." The vid screen displayed Klaus' suggestion.

Hiroshi offered, "They didn't have the fire power to take the village by force." The vid screen displayed Hiroshi's suggestion below Klaus's.

And so it went for the next half-hour. We recorded eleven suggested reasons for the hoax and then ran out of ideas. For the next hour we discussed each of the eleven in detail. Some were discounted quickly, others took a long time to discuss. We finally finished.

We decided the most likely reason was a combination of several suggestions. The hoax at the *Blue Streak* village was a dry run for a larger operation. It was a test to see what effect the avatar dragon would have on humans. There was nothing of significance at the village to justify such an attack. The five shuttles could have been possible targets, but they were low tech compared to the *Golden Dragon's* shuttles.

The result of the dragon attack had the desired result, the five *Blue Streak* shuttles quickly left their village and headed to New Jerusalem and its target rich environment. There was some speculation that New Jerusalem was the only large city left on Earth. If the *Golden Dragon's* goal was world domination, New Jerusalem would be the next likely target.

It was decided that we needed to prepare for war against an enemy with superior technology. Dr. Sanborn was tasked with developing techniques to see through any avatars they might use to distract us. We needed to determine if we'd be fighting only shuttles or if *Golden Dragon's* mothership was out there in synchronous orbit. We'd have to search space above East Asia to be sure.

Lastly, we wanted to know if we would be fighting humans, AI controlled robots or androids, or a combination of both.

No one had any idea how to determine the nature of our enemy.

Search for the Mothership—Major Doug Fleharty

Shuttle Sierra was still configured for synchronous orbit flight. I made contact with the same crew that went searching for the *Blue Streak* mothership. Using the same crew made sense; they had all the necessary experience. Commander Koyama was the only one from the original crew who wasn't going with us. He was responsible for several other operations. I added another marine to take his place.

It took two days to get the shuttle outfitted and weaponized. I held a preflight briefing with the crew an hour before launch. We boarded Sierra on schedule and had a routine launch. We achieved LEO as planned and began searching for the mothership as we approached East Asia. It was tally-ho on the second orbit. When we came around the next time we began our burn to synchronous orbit. The ride was routine, except you never get used to a high G ride for several hours. It's just pure pain. I really wished we could find some inertia dampeners.

We shut down our propulsion system several hours from our target and glided weightless until we were about a hundred miles farther behind the mothership and fifty miles below her. We located a large piece of space junk and maneuvered behind it, hiding us from being detected. In the lower orbit we were moving slightly faster than the mothership. It took us almost two hours to get into the proper alignment at which point we scanned her with passive sensors and kept our stealth shields at full power. The first thing I noticed was the golden dragon painted on the side of the hull extending from stem to stern. It was a brilliant gold.

She was active, fully operational. She had two shuttle bays on the port side of the ship, both had their doors open and we counted locations for ten shuttles in each bay. There were three shuttles in one bay and two in the other. All were armed with laser cannons and rockets. The burning question I had was why hadn't the mothership and her shuttle chicks not remained at Proxima B as planned? It occurred to me that maybe she never left Earth orbit. Maybe something happened to keep her here. Perhaps some type of malfunction locked her into synchronous orbit forever.

As I was musing over these possibilities, Jack, our copilot, said, "I think they've spotted us. There's a shuttle approaching us slowly from below."

"Shut down all systems including life support," I said immediately. "Use your suit's air supply. How far away?" I asked.

"Looks like she's coming up from Earth. About a hundred miles and slowing to enter the rear bay," Jack answered.

"Trish, make us look like a derelict, tumbling and twisting. Minimum maneuvering jets. Just like we planned."

"Aye sir," Trish replied as very gradually Sierra began to tumble.

The approaching shuttle continued on its way to the hanger bay. At its closest point, active scanners began to ping us. I hoped with all systems shut down we didn't look like any type of threat. We continued to drift past the mothership and watched the shuttle through the windscreen as it touched down in the shuttle bay. When we were several hundred miles from the mothership, we used our maneuvering jets to initiate our descent. We turned on all our systems, beginning with life support, and brought our reactor back to life.

Our trip back to LEO and finally to New Jerusalem was uneventful. I said a prayer of thanks and went to report our findings to the Tribunal.

Preparing for War–Rear Admiral David Lawrence

Doug had just left the Tribunal office after briefing us on his mission. We all sat quietly for a few minutes pondering the ramifications of this new information. It seemed to me another piece of the puzzle had been turned over, however, we couldn't see how it fit in with the other puzzle pieces.

I looked around the conference table at the other three Tribunal members. I noticed Governor Stewart seemed to be in pain. "John, are you all right?" I asked.

He shook his head, "No, I think I'm having a heart…"

He never finished his sentence. He tried to rise, but his legs would not support him and he fell back in his chair. He moaned loudly once and then was still.

Paul, or John, I had a difficult time telling which one, ran out to our lobby area and was back in an instant with the medic on duty. The medic scanned the governor and then quickly pulled a pneumatic injector from his bag as the apostle ripped open his shirt. The medic injected what I hoped was a medicine which would keep him alive. He began CPR, but we all realized it was hopeless. He was dead.

A few minutes later, Dr. Song ran into our office, scanned the governor again and shook her head. "He's gone. I'm so sorry. There was nothing we could do to save him." She fought to compose herself, it was a losing battle. I put my arms around her as she began to weep. "Please," she said to me, "let me tell his wife and children. We were all such close friends. I can't believe he's gone."

When Simon heard of the governor's passing, he was momentarily shocked. However, being Simon, he was suspicious and pushed for an autopsy. He told the Tribunal, "We stand on the brink of war again.

We face an enemy with almost magical powers. I think it only prudent not to accept any death as due to natural causes."

He was right, of course. An autopsy was performed, but not by Dr. Song. She said, "I will assign my best surgeon to do the procedure. I'll observe, of course. I just can't bring myself to cut my old friend."

The autopsy was performed and it turned out the cause of death was a ruptured aorta. Apparently, recent physicals had indicated there might be some thinning of the aorta wall, however, nothing was conclusive.

Dr. Song reviewed all the medical reports of each annual physical immediately after they were performed. She did that routinely for each one of the Tribunal. She had cautioned the governor to avoid stressful activities. Stress causes the blood pressure to increase. High blood pressure over prolonged periods of time will lead to a rupture in any artery that has significantly thinned. He had been prescribed meds to control his blood pressure. His wife indicated he took the meds religiously. There was only so much the meds could help.

The governor's death was by natural causes. A funeral was held, it was a beautiful service. Paul and John presided.

It was a shame that we didn't have the time to grieve as we should have. We had to prepare for the *Golden Dragon's* attack. The widow and her children were forced to grieve alone. Of course, Miriam, Anna and Soo Song visited the family as much as possible. That helped a lot, however I felt we should have done more to honor all the many things he had done to integrate the people of *Hope* with New Jerusalem.

Our first order of business was to select a replacement for the governor. We nominated Dr. Song. My wife, Miriam, said it was about time a woman was part of the Tribunal. I told her not to get too excited, we hadn't asked her to join us yet.

The next day, we sent her a formal invitation. Her initial response was, "Are you kidding me? This is a joke, right?"

We sent our assurances. Fifteen minutes later she showed up at the Tribunal office with our invitation in hand. The three of us just happened to be in session when she barged in unannounced. "Is this invitation the real deal? It smells of a practical joke, something my husband could have done."

The twins sat mute as I answered. "It's written on Tribunal stationary isn't?"

"Please, just answer my question."

"Yes, Soo. It's real. The three of us feel you are the best person to replace the governor. Just so you know, one of the first duties of a new Tribunal member is to recommend a person to replace themselves, hopefully in the distant future. Governor Stewart recommended you some time ago."

At the sound of the governor's name, her legs buckled and John (or Paul) jumped up and helped her into a chair. "I'm so sorry. I'm acting like a baby. Just hearing his name causes me to become weak in the knees."

The other twin, at least I thought it was the other one, it's so hard to tell them apart, offered her a glass of water. She took a sip of water and said, "How long do I have to decide?"

"Take all the time you need," I answered. "Ten or fifteen minutes, no rush."

She began to choke on the sip and one of the twins patted her on the back and frowned at me.

When she had stopped coughing she said to me, "What a joker you are."

"Nope, that call sign has been taken. My call sign is Arab." I paused and noticed her confusion. "Like Lawrence of Arabia?"

She looked even more confused. "What's a call sign?" she asked with a blank stare. That lasted about five seconds and she began to giggle. "Gotcha, didn't I?" she snorted which caused the rest of us to begin laughing as well.

When we finally composed ourselves, she said, "I'd be honored to accept your invitation. I pray I will be able to contribute half as much as my dear friend."

"Whew," exclaimed John and Paul simultaneously. "I guess we can throw away the list of other candidates."

Soo's head snapped to glare at them, wadded up her invitation and threw it at the closest one. It bounced off his forehead onto the floor. She rose from her chair and headed for the door. At the last moment she turned and glared at all of us and in her best Spanish accent said, "Invitation? I don't need no stinking invitation." She closed the door behind her.

We looked at each other and broke out laughing hysterically. "She's going to fit in just fine," I said when I caught my breath. "Just fine."

We all met the next morning at nine for our daily meeting. It was all business now. Dr. Song looked very professional in dark pants, a beige turtle neck sweater with a gold chain around her neck. I think it was the first time I had ever seen her in heels, not too high, but very stylish. The men were dressed as always, in what I heard historians refer to as business casual. By default, I had become the defacto speaker for the group. The Moses had been our first speaker, followed by the governor and now me.

Every morning we began by going through an agenda of issues dealing with New Jerusalem problems or issues. The last half of the meeting was set aside to discuss the pending war with *Golden Dragon*. We usually asked Hiroshi, Simon and Dr. Sanborn to attend for that part of the meeting.

We went quickly through the nine agenda items. We took a short break when finished. The three men showed up right on time. After getting a drink and a pastry they joined us at the conference table.

I led off the discussion. "I think the *Golden Dragon* mothership is a wild card. It may not even take part in the war, leaving it to her shuttles to do all the dirty work. I mean it can't get too involved from a synchronous orbit, that's over twenty thousand miles in space. If it drops to a LEO, it would only be over us for a few minutes of each orbit which would severely limit its involvement. I'm inclined to rule it out and focus on the shuttles and whatever troops they can land. What are your thoughts?"

"I tend to agree," replied Hiroshi. "On the other hand, it might remain in synchronous orbit and move until it's directly over New Jerusalem to better support the shuttles."

"Any other comments regarding the mothership?" I asked. There were none.

Next I said, "If you were the *Golden Dragon*, how would you begin an attack on us?"

Dr. Sanborn answered immediately, "I'd begin with what I know works. They have to feel pretty good about how the entire *Blue Streak* village bolted after the dragon show. For us, I wouldn't try the morphing dragon again. I'd try something different." He paused for a moment and then continued, "I'd flood the sky with images of shuttles, even though we know they have at most twenty shuttles, they could make it look like a lot more. Their avatars are so real looking, we wouldn't know which ones were fakes. We could waste a lot of time and armament going after fake targets. The same could be said for landed troops. They could make it appear they have a lot more than they really do. I think I have to come up with a fast way to identify avatars from the real thing."

"Simon, what about our troop deployment?" I asked.

"I believe their main target has to be the ancient's lab. If they are truly limited to artificial intelligence beings they would have no interest in structures like buildings or things that human's would go to war for. The lab is full of computers and supporting hardware that an AI would have an interest in. Do you agree Dr. Sanborn?"

Dr. Sanborn nodded his head in agreement. "Absolutely, Simon, I can't imagine artificial life having any interest in tractors or canned food. They'd want the high tech stuff. I'm just not sure if our systems are really all that high tech compared to what they already have."

"You may be right," conceded Simon. "They'd not find it worth their while to raid our out-of-date computing systems. However I think they would need to check it out before they decide if it's worthwhile. Since the last war, the lab has been reorganized with shelters for our people on one side and all of the computers, weapons and general supplies and equipment on the other. I would place the oldest computers closest to the lab entrance and the newest computer systems and excess weapons as far away from the entrance as possible. I would then booby trap the main entrance in the hopes of destroying as many of the enemy as possible when they attempt to evaluate our computers. I would place a large contingency of marines and protectors to guard our families in the shelter area and the remainder of our troops throughout the city and the suburbs to slow the enemy down if they decide to destroy our structures. I will have a more detailed breakdown of troop allotment for tomorrow's meeting."

I had a thought and threw it out for discussion. "Does anyone think it would be worth the risk to see if *Golden Dragon* actually moved into the *Blue Streak* village or if it was only a bluff?"

Hiroshi responded first, "Yes, it would help us determine their motive for the attack. It would be a quick and easy way to see if they really wanted the village or to just get the people to abandon it without a fight."

And so it went for the remainder of the hour.

We came away with some assignments and a rough strategy on how we would deal the enemy when they attacked.

Recon of the Village—Commander Hiroshi Koyama

Later that morning, Shuttle Sierra launched to determine the status of the *Blue Streak's* abandoned village. It was an out-and-back mission, info gathering only. Avoid contact if possible, return home the same day, have dinner with the wife and kids.

Shuttle Sierra was staffed with the same crew as the last mission to Europe. The plan was to check all the other villages we had discovered on our first trip and end up at *Blue Streak* city. We were to record everything, then beat it back to New Jerusalem.

Trish launched us into the same sub-orbital flight profile with the same nasty Gs. As I lay in my acceleration couch barely able to breathe, I wondered if inertia dampeners were even a possibility.

As we began our long glide back into the atmosphere we were checking to see if anything looked different. Darin, our mission analyst, assured me everything looked the same except for one important feature; he couldn't detect any people, either alive or dead. They were just gone.

As we reached our surveillance altitude and began our more detailed investigation, it was the same story. "This is just creepy, skipper," commented Darin. "It's like the beginning of an old horror vid. Where did they all go?"

We slowed as we approached our target village. Everything was intact just as it was the last time we were here; the ruins of the church had not changed. We did a slow circle of the village just to be sure.

We were operating in stealth mode, preparing to return home when our copilot shouted, "Contact, boggy at three o'clock, ten thousand feet, closing fast!"

"Do you recognize it, Jack? Is it a *Golden Dragon* shuttle?" I asked.

"Unknown," he answered. "It's partially cloaked, going in and out of stealth like it may be malfunctioning."

I ordered Trish to take us down and land us close to a large barn maintaining our own stealth shield. "Any indication it spotted us?"

"Not yet, skipper," replied Darin, "I think it's having problems…It's propulsion system just went off line…It's going to crash…Really close to us!"

We heard the impact as the craft crashed into the ground. There was no explosion, just the sickening sound of metal being torn apart. When it stopped I ordered Trish, "Shut down all systems and open the hatch. We need to examine the wreck." Darin and I and the two marines hurried outside.

It was the size of a small shuttle. It was really banged up from the crash, but we managed to get the hatch open and went inside. There were seats for six, all of them were empty. What really freaked me out was that there was no place for a pilot or copilot. All the things you would expect to see on a shuttle were missing; no flight controls, no propulsion system controls, no coms, nothing, completely bare.

I did a quick scan of the inside cabin with the vid recorder and then handed it to one of the marines and told him to go outside and take pictures of everything, especially the propulsion area.

Darin and I took our laser torches and began cutting up all the bulkhead panels looking for some type of computer interface equipment. We came across two boxes about the size of a large duffel bag. One of them looked fried, but the other one looked intact. We took them both, meeting the marines coming around the other side of the wreck. "Got it," said the marine with the vid recorder. We hurried back to Sierra.

"Fire it up, Trish," I yelled. "We need to get out of here *muy pronto*. We're going to have lots of company to check on their shuttle. I don't want to leave a trace of us when they arrive."

Trish, as always, had beat me to it. I could hear various systems already coming online and lots of panel lights switching from red to green. As I strapped into my seat, Darin slid in besides me and said, "Really, skipper? *Muy pronto?* You're Japanese. Japanese men don't speak Spanish!" He started laughing as he fastened his harness.

The hatch made a hissing noise as it sealed and Trish yelled over her shoulder, "Launching now."

I stared at Darin as Sierra lifted off, skimming over the ground until we reached the river. We followed the river just high enough not to cause a wake as we continued to accelerate. I asked, "Did I really say *muy pronto?*"

He nodded and waited for an explanation. I sheepishly said, "My wife, Anna, is taking a Spanish class at the college. I've been drilling her on some Spanish phrases. I guess it just slipped out." Everyone sat quietly as we began our climb to sub-orbital altitude, however I could see smirks on many of the crew's faces.

The rest of the flight was uneventful. As far as we knew, we made it home without being detected. We comm'd ahead to give them a heads up on what happened and asked Dr. Sanborn to meet us as we touched down. I wanted him to determine the function of the electronic equipment we scavenged. He sounded as happy as a kid with a new giz wiz toy.

I took the vid records of the crashed shuttle and headed for the Tribunal office.

There was a full house waiting for me when I arrived.

Golden Dragon Shuttle Analysis–The Tribunal

When Hiroshi came through the door he was met by an expanded version of the Tribunal. The two extras were SSP Simon and Dr. John Sanborn. Actually, John was a little late, he wanted to get his people working on the electronic packages from the crashed shuttle.

Hiroshi gave us a quick briefing on the nature of their original mission, and then followed up with the crash. He summarized the mission first. "We flew in along the same route we used on a previous mission to find the *Blue Streak* village. On the first mission we saw several smaller villages along the way, they were agrarian communities living off the land. When we reached the *Blue Streak* village, it was much larger than those we first spotted; around five hundred people with mechanized equipment and at least five shuttles.

"On this last mission everything was the same except for one important point, there were no humans sighted anywhere, neither alive nor dead. We saw livestock herds and wild animals in the forest areas, but no humans anywhere. Of course the people from the *Blue Streak* village escaped to New Jerusalem before this occurred.

"We completed our mission and were preparing to head home when an enemy shuttle was spotted. It was in obvious distress and heading towards us. We were in deep stealth mode with all our systems shut down. I don't think we were seen. After the crash, my crew did a quick inspection of the shuttle, both inside and out. All of that was vid recorded. We will show the vid to you momentarily. I took the vids of the interior of the shuttle, then handed the vid recorder to one of our marine escorts and had him record the exterior. While they were busy recording, Lieutenant Darin Davis and myself tore out the interior bulkheads looking for anything electronic."

I stood and said, "Thank you Hiroshi, any questions before we see the vid recording?" There were none. I turned toward the vid screen and said, "Play vid record 722A."

There was about fifteen minutes of recording, but several times we were asked to rerun certain sections and asked for clarity. The first question was, "Where do the pilots sit?" The second was, "Where are the flight controls?"

It was very hard to believe the shuttle had no pilots nor any visible controls or instruments pilots would use. "How do they fly it?" was the next question asked.

Dr. Sanborn had just entered the room. Before he could sit down he said, "I can answer that. I'm almost certain the shuttles are flown by the computers in the mothership. We just finished our preliminary inspection of the electronic equipment Hiroshi and his crew salvaged from the crashed shuttle.

"We believe their purpose was to serve as downlink receivers. Think of the AI computers aboard the mothership as a hive-mind controlling all of their shuttles. I believe the same AI computer system also controls the flight of the mothership and everything in her. It must be a computer very far advanced from ours. Perhaps it's even an organic computer system."

Another question was asked, "We saw six seats that appeared to be designed for normal human beings. Does that imply there are humans aboard the mothership?"

The admiral replied, "Perhaps, but I think that unlikely. The seats may be for android creatures that have the same physical features as humans. They could be autonomous beings or driven by the AI computer system aboard the mothership. It could be a combination of the two."

The room went quiet as everyone was attempting to absorb the implications of all the new information.

Dr. Song stood and said, "The findings from this mission are incredible and in many instances difficult to integrate into a battle strategy. The Tribunal wishes to recognize the outstanding performance of the crew of Shuttle Sierra for their critical discoveries. We will adjourn now but will meet again tomorrow morning after we have had a chance to consider all that was presented here this evening. Thank you all for coming and your contributions. This concludes are meeting. We hope to see you all here tomorrow."

The Surprise Visit—Commander Henry White

I'd just finished putting Junior to bed. I was reading him a story, one of my favorites, about a little runt of a guy who became a champion weightlifter. I'd just gotten to the good part when I realized he'd fallen asleep. What a joy my children are to me. Ten years ago I never thought I'd ever get married let alone have children. But look at me now with three kids who are truly the love of my life. Of course, Soo Song is at the top of the love list. I can't believe that woman actually loves me.

She'd gone to bed early tonight, exhausted from holding down two full time jobs. After Senior Healer Johnson got demoted, Soo was promoted becoming the director of all of New Jerusalem's hospitals and medical centers. Then a few weeks ago, with the passing of the governor, she was appointed to be a member of the Tribunal. I don't know how she finds time to do everything. I decided to help wherever I could. I didn't realize how tough being a house husband was going to be.

I checked in on the other two kids and peaked in on Soo. She was snoring softly, so I quietly closed the door and headed out to the living room to watch a vid of an old-time power lifting tournament I'd come across.

As I rounded the corner from the hall to the front room, I stopped dead in my tracks. Sitting on my recliner was a beautiful black woman I had never seen before.

She smiled at me and said in a very melodic voice, "Good evening, commander. Hope your evening went well. You look tired so I won't take long."

I quickly scanned the doors and adjacent rooms to see if she brought any friends. All the doors were dead bolted and the rooms were empty.

"How did you get into my house?" I asked in my most menacing voice.

Apparently it didn't impress her. "I'm afraid I don't have time for those types of details. I've come to give you a message, a very important message."

I scowled at her and began to walk toward her. "You're not real, are you? You're some kind of avatar. You need to get out of my house and never come back."

She stood and closed the distance between us. Before I could get my hands up she hit me in the solar plexus harder than I had ever been hit before. The force of the strike sent my diaphragm into spasms. I couldn't breathe. I felt like I was on the brink of passing out. I stumbled backwards and fell to the floor on my back. She squatted next to me and asked, "Is that real enough for you, Henry? Here's the message, big boy: Surrender or die. You'll get more instructions tomorrow. Stay tuned."

She started to walk toward the patio door, then stopped and turned back to me. "It must be really humiliating for a man of your size and strength to be knocked down by two different women. Have a good night." She turned back to the doors and walked right through them like they weren't even there. After a few steps her image began to fade, a moment later she had vanished.

I lay there trying to breathe when Soo came out of the bedroom and saw me on the floor. "What's all the racket ab... Henry what happened, are you okay!?"

I nodded and was finally able to catch my breath. I looked up at Soo and said, "I just got my butt kicked by another woman."

Soo helped me onto the couch and had me lay down. She began to check me out to make sure nothing was broken or torn. As she worked she asked me, "Who was the woman? Anybody I'd know?"

I shook my head. "No, it was a very attractive black woman, or so she appeared. I thought she was an avatar from *Golden Dragon*, like the girl Klaus and Marta saw, all smoke and mirrors, except this one hit like a mule kicks." I began coughing and ended up vomiting a little. There was blood in the vomit.

"That's it," my wife said with a look of concern on her face. "You're going to the hospital right now."

She turned to get her com, but I grabbed her arm, "Wait, please. She gave me a message. She said, 'surrender or die.' We're supposed to get instructions tomorrow."

The expression on Soo's face changed from one of concern to one of terror. She ran for her com. "Dave this is Soo. Sorry to bother you so late but we have an emergency, actually two emergencies. I have to take Henry to the hospital, he was injured in a fight with an alien woman… No, I'm not joking," she said angrily. "She told Henry we have to surrender or die, instructions to follow tomorrow."

Somewhere between our home and the hospital, I passed out. I guess she hurt me more than I thought. When I regained conscious, it was the next morning. I couldn't believe she hurt me that badly. I looked under the sheet and saw I had a large bandage over my abdomen. Yellow, black and purple bruises encircled the bandage. *Damn!* I thought to myself. *She really messed me up.*

A nurse came into my room and I asked for my wife. She told me Dr. Song was in a Tribunal meeting and would get with me as soon as the meeting was over. She checked my vitals and got ready to leave. She headed for the door but stopped, turned back and asked me. "How did you get hurt so badly? I just came on shift and nobody seems to know what happened to you. Were you in an accident?"

I shook my head. "No, not an accident. Someone hit me in the stomach."

"My goodness!" she exclaimed. "He must have been a giant to cause so much damage."

I shook my head again. "No, it was a woman, smaller than you."

Her mouth dropped in shock. She quickly closed it and I saw the beginning of a smile. She began to turn for the door.

At first I was puzzled by the smile, but then it dawned on me. I shouted after her, "It wasn't Dr. Song who hit me. A complete stranger…"

She was out the door. I don't think she heard me. *How embarrassing.*

Soo came into my room about an hour later. She had an entourage with her. "Your attacker was an avatar after all. John, please show him the vid from our security system." I'd forgotten Tribunal members all had security surveillance wherever they went, including their homes.

Dr. Sanborn stepped up and showed me the vid with the filters applied. It looked like I was speaking with a hovering watermelon. As I walked forward it moved towards me and a metal battering ram slammed into my stomach.

Hiroshi was leaning over John's shoulder. He winced in sympathetic pain as the ram struck me. He looked up at me and shook his head. "That had to really hurt. Sorry for your pain, man. You really took one for the team. But look on the bright side. You weren't beaten up by another woman. This time it was a watermelon."

I ignored Hiroshi's sense of humor, turned toward John and asked, "How did she get the watermelon out of the room. I saw her walk through a solid door. So how did she get the watermelon outside?"

"You've got it backwards, Henry," answered John. "The watermelon is real. Just like it generated the avatar, it created the illusion they went through the door without opening. Look at the vid with the filters on." I saw the watermelon move towards the door, open it and close it after it had passed through.

"I'll be damned! Those watermelons are sneaky little bastards," I exclaimed.

Admiral Lawrence hadn't spoken. Now he came forward and looked at me with sadness in his eyes, "Henry, I'm so sorry this happened. We are up against a very different type of enemy. The Tribunal, without the knowledge of Soo, voted," he reached into his pocket and bought out a small box. He opened it towards me and took out an award, a Purple Heart. "Commander White, you are awarded this medal for the injuries you received while in battle against our enemy." He stepped forward and pinned the medial onto my hospital gown. He stepped back and he and Hiroshi came to attention and saluted me. I answered with a salute of my own. The best I could do while lying in bed. Before I could thank them, the admiral continued, "For coming out of retirement and serving the military needs of our community, you are here by promoted to the rank of captain." They saluted again as Soo pinned the silver eagles next to my purple heart.

After my three friends left, Soo sat on the edge of my bed and held my hand. "You're lucking to be alive. John told me he calculated the ram hit you with enough force to break a concrete block. It kind of messed you up inside. Quite a bite of trauma to your abdominal muscles, no rips or tears, however a lot of bruising. The problem is internal bleeding. We need to do some exploratory work to see where the blood is coming from. I'm afraid you are going to have to stay in the hospital for a few days."

I started to protest. "I can't stay here for days. I've got to take care of our kids so you can do the important work. I promise, I'll take it eas…"

She began to tear up. That scared me. I'd never seen her cry, except when she messed me up during her self-defense demo over a decade ago.

"Baby, this is serious. It needs to be taken care of now. Anna and Miriam said they would rotate taking care of the kids during the day, I'll be home in the evenings…"

"But the war is com…"

"Hush your mouth, husband," her was voice soft and quivering. "Others will take care of the war. Henry, your injury is life threatening. The longer you wait, the more likely you won't survive."

She stopped talking, tears began streaming down her cheeks and she made no effort to wipe them away. After a moment she added, "And baby, I can't survive without you, so you need to get this done now."

I put my arms around her and pulled her to me. Her tears had turned to sobbing. Now I was sobbing too. I rocked her in my arms to comfort her, ignoring the pain in my gut as best I could. I whispered in her ear, "It's going to be okay, my love. I'll be okay. Whatever you want, I'll do it. Please don't cry."

She sat up and I wiped away her tears. She leaned forward and kissed me on the mouth, not a passionate kiss, but a warm, wonderful kiss filled with love. She sniffed a few times then smiled at me, "Thank you, baby. I love you so much."

She leaned forward and gave me another kiss then stood up. "I'm going to order your procedure right now. Unfortunately I have to go back to work after that. I'll come to see you as soon as I can. I'll bring the kids."

She blew me a last kiss and hurried from the room. My stomach was really starting to burn.

War Planning–Speaker Admiral Lawrence

The morning after the attack on Henry we put together a war council. Its participants consisted of The Tribunal, The Ruling Council from *Blue Streak*, Commander Koyama and SSP Simon. For this meeting we also invited Miriam Lawrence and Anna Koyama who had been given responsibility for getting the New Jerusalem citizens and immigrants into the shelters.

The first order of business was to inform everyone as to what took place the previous evening. I turned the meeting over to Dr. Song and Dr. Sanborn. Everyone was stunned by what was presented. Klaus said, "It's just like the girl at our polka, only without the dragon. I believe that means it is coming soon, perhaps as early as today."

Dr. Song finished by telling everyone Commander White was still in the hospital and would need surgery to stop the internal bleeding.

Next Dr. Sanborn reported the *Golden Dragon* mothership was now in synchronous orbit over New Jerusalem. He said he believed the mothership needed line-of-sight to her shuttle fleet in order to control them efficiently. He believed the shuttles may have some limited autonomous control, however the mothership computer, he referred to it as the Hive Queen, was needed to coordinate their movements. He indicated *Golden Dragon* could have as many as twenty shuttles. He didn't believe the small shuttle that crashed was part of the war fleet. It had no weapons or stealth capabilities.

Miriam and Anna followed Dr. Sanborn with a report on the shelter status. Miriam began by showing vids of children of all ages entering their temporary classrooms in the ancient's lab. The lab's shelter accommodations had been expanded as the city's population had grown. This growth also included the suburbs and the immigrant dormitories.

She was about to introduce Anna, when there was a loud knock on the door. The security vid showing the outside hallway in front of the conference room door revealed two marines lying on the floor and three men standing in front of the door. The two protectors and two more marines inside the conference room hurried to the doors with weapons at the ready. One of the protectors touched the speaker button near the door and said, "Please identify yourselves and state your business."

One of the three men said, "We have important business with the war council."

The protector replied, "This is a classified meeting. In order to attend you must have the proper security clearance and received an invitation."

There was an audible sign and the voice said, "This is becoming tediously boring. Please stand back from the doors."

Everyone in the conference room was on their feet and moving back from the door as far as they could go, anticipating an explosive breach of the steel door. Instead there was a *snick* as locking bolts slid back and the door opened wide. Our guards looked paralyzed as the three men strolled into the room.

There were gasps of recognition as the first man said, "Hello my friends. It's so good to see you all again." It was The Moses, dressed in his ceremonial robes.

No one spoke for what seemed like an eternity, then I turned to the second man. "Governor?" I exclaimed. "You can't be here. You're dead!"

He smiled and nodded his head. "I was dead, but I'm alive again, just as The Moses and Pastor Luther died and are alive again."

SSP Simon was walking towards the creature who called himself The Moses. He stopped in front of him and loudly said, "This creature is not The Moses. He is not even flesh and blood, he is smoke and mirrors. Look, I can stick my hand right thro…"

His hand came to rest on The Moses' shoulder. Simon seemed puzzled for a moment and stepped back. Then he began to smile. "Now I understand, you are not an avatar like the others we have seen. You have no watermelon inside a projected image. No, you are the next level, an android made to look like my Moses. You are an abomination, a fraud. My Moses was murdered and cut into pieces during an autopsy, all his organs removed, even his brain was taken out and sliced into thin strips."

Simon grabbed the man's arm and raised it high above his head. The sleeve of his robe slid down revealing his bare arm. Simon shouted to everyone in the room, "Look everyone. It looks human, but I promise you it is not." He had picked up a fork from the buffet table and now he sunk the tines of the fork deeply into the man's forearm. The man yelled in pain and jerked his arm away. As he pulled the fork out of his arm, streams of blood began to flow down onto the floor.

Someone grabbed a napkin and pressed it against the wound to stem the bleeding. The man stood up straight and yelled, "Simon, you fool, I told you I had died! This is my glorified body. Look how fast I heel."

He removed the napkin from the four puncture wounds. The bleeding had stopped and as Simon watched the wounds began to close. In less than a minute they were gone. It was as if he had never been wounded.

Simon was confused, but he refused to believe this was his Moses. "You are a lie, a fabrication, not a resurrected Moses. You are a demon disguised as my Moses. No one is resurrected until judgment day. How about I kill you now and see if you come back again?"

As he began to reach for his weapon, Hiroshi grabbed his arms and restrained him. "Not yet, Simon. Not now. We need to hear what he proposes."

Simon struggled to free himself, but Hiroshi was younger and stronger. He could not reach his weapon. "Please let me kill him," he begged.

I stepped up behind them, leaned in and whispered into Simon's ear, "When the time is right, he's all yours. I promise."

While this was going on, Klaus, Marta and others from the *Blue Streak* Ruling Council were moving toward the third man speaking rapidly in German. Marta reached out and took his hand. In English she said, "Look, he is our pastor. He is solid, his flesh is warm, I smell his favorite cologne. He is real! How can this be?" She wailed, "It's a miracle. A miracle, I tell you." Her eyes rolled upward and she began to swoon, Klaus caught her and carried her to the couch.

After the shock and awe was over, we wearily returned to our seats and allowed them to say their piece. The man who looked like Moses was their spokesman. "Next Sabbath is judgment day. Our Lord and Savior will return to Earth just as it is written in the Book of Revelation. All will be made clear at that time. I suggest you get your house in order before He returns in the clouds of glory."

They turned and walked out of the conference room, then out of the Temple to the plaza. A tractor beam captured them and they floated upward until they were out of sight.

Miriam was still standing at the podium as we took our seats. When everyone was settled in she said, "Well, I didn't see *that* coming. Life keeps getting weirder and weirder."

"Amen to that," replied Paul and John simultaneously.

That produced limited nervous laughter.

Miriam turned to her husband, "My admiral, I surrender the podium to you. I have no idea what to say next."

I stood and said, "I accept the podium, my wife. Have a seat."

I scanned the room for a moment before speaking again. I saw a mixture of reactions to what we just experienced. "How many people think the three men we just saw were actually who they claimed to be?" Only a few hands went up, one was Marta's.

"Okay, how many people think they were creations of the Hive Queen?" A few more hands went up, but not many more.

"Finally, how many are unsure of what they saw?" The majority of hands were raised. "I'm also in the last category. Does anyone have any idea of anything we haven't considered?"

After a short pause, Dr Sanborn raised his hand. I surrendered the podium to him. He said, "Does everyone know what a simulacrum is?" Only a few hands were raised. He nodded and said, "It's a name given to artificial life forms. The key word is *life.* It's an artificially created living being. There are numerous paths this can take. It can start with the DNA of an actual human being which is grown into a living creature, but its mind would be blank, no memories at all, no personality. Simon demonstrated the creature that claimed to be The Moses had a human body. As far as his mind goes, I see two options, perhaps three. They could have combined the human body with an organic AI minicomputer programmed to simulate The Moses. They could have used the existing brain and downloaded The Moses' memories. A third option would be to use a combination of the two. I believe the first option is the most likely."

"Interesting theory John," I said. "I have a hard time understanding how they could grow a human body to maturity in the matter of a few days. Is that even possible?"

"I believe it is admiral," he replied. "In studying the information on the databases regarding *Golden Dragon,* I came across an article about how Chinese scientists had developed a process called accelerated maturation. They referred to an experiment where they took a hundred fertilized embryos and subjected them to the accelerated maturation process. In three days they successfully produced eighty-nine percent of the embryos into mature adults."

"Wow," said Dr. Song. "That's disturbing on so many levels. What about their cognitive functions?"

"Their minds were blank, of course. However, they did reference another paper regarding research on infusing blank minds with memories and personalities," answered Dr. Sanborn.

"Really!" exclaimed Soo. "That's even more disturbing. Were you able to access the referenced paper?"

"Unfortunately, no." He paused, pursed his lips together for a moment as if deciding to say more. He shrugged, before continuing. "If they can do all this, I strongly believe the simulacrums would feel they were the persons they were designed to be. The fake Moses could truly believe he's the real deal, raised from the dead in a glorified body. I can't wait to see our Lord and Savior." Nobody laughed.

I stood up and said, "Let's review by summarizing what we now think we know." I raised my index finger and said, "They have three, maybe four, types of humanoid appearing creatures: avatars, androids, simulacrums, and possibly real humans. I only mentioned the last category for completeness. Does anyone have any more categories of humanoids to suggest?"

"Why did you include androids?" asked Dr. Song. "As far as I know we haven't seen any."

"Good point, Soo," I replied. "It's more of a gut feeling than anything else. It seems like a logical step between the avatars and the simulacrums. I seriously doubt there are any remaining humans amongst them. It takes a lot to maintain a human and they are difficult to control, usually unpredictable."

I held up a second finger. "Next are the shuttles, possibly as many as twenty based on the number of parking spaces in *Golden Dragon's* shuttle bays. We believe all of them are flown by the Hive Queen computer aboard the mothership. In fact, I believe everything they've got is controlled by the mothership. She is the supreme commander. There are no autonomous entities."

Hiroshi jumped in, "Kill the queen and all of *Golden Dragon* dies with her."

"Exactly!" I exclaimed, "How do we destroy a ship that remains overhead watching our every move? A ship so far away it would take several hours to reach her. A ship that's considerably more technically advanced than us. A ship that bristling with offensive and defensive weapons."

Again, Hiroshi interrupted, "From above. We attack her from above with a nuclear bomb."

"Absolutely not!" shouted Dr. Song. "To date they haven't killed anyone from New Jerusalem that we know of. Yes, a lot of people are missing in Europe, but that doesn't mean they're dead, or if they are, the *Golden Dragon* is responsible for their deaths. I agree with Hiroshi, shutting down the Hive Queen would end the war. Can't we do it without nuclear weapons? Wouldn't it be to our advantage to shut down the Hive Queen and bring her back to New Jerusalem? It would end the war as well as offer us incredible improvements in our computing systems. If we could reprogram it, think of all the possibilities."

Everyone sat quietly considering what Dr. Song just offered. Her plan had merit, a lot of merit. However, it was a much higher risk approach. "Ok people," I said. "We need to do a risk-benefit analysis and we need to do it right now. No matter which path we choose, it's going to take a lot of planning and we don't have a lot of time. Let's get busy."

We brought in our best strategic planners and got to work immediately. Twelve hours later we had a plan.

The Last Sabbath–Apostles John and Paul

Seeing the simulacrum of The Moses really upset us. Under other circumstances we would never believe it possible it wasn't him. And yet the things he said were a little off. Listening to our group's comments after the three simulacrums left us was like watching a science fiction vid or perhaps a horror vid. All the talk about avatars, androids and simulacrums seemed so bizarre, as well as a Hive Queen controlling everything and a possible nuclear war.

We began an intensive review of the second coming of Jesus and Judgment Day. Our main resources were the Book of Revelation written by the Apostle John and First and Second Thessalonians written by the Apostle Paul, not us, the original apostles. We wanted to be prepared to refute anything presented that was not in accordance with scripture.

The admiral had cautioned us not to believe everything the fake Moses said. The announcement of the second coming might well be a misdirection to throw us off, but he wanted us to be prepared, just in case.

The entire Temple area was undergoing a complete upgrade of surveillance equipment and defensive systems. We assumed the fake Jesus would come to the Sanctuary to make his judgment of good and evil. Of course no one was going to be allowed in the Sanctuary during any of the activities, except us. We were to be hosts for whoever showed up, lucky us.

Most of New Jerusalem's citizens would be sequestered in the ancient's lab shelters. What ever happened would be recorded and made available in real time on all the shelter's vids.

The only ones not in the shelters were the protectors, SP and military troops, all were heavily armed and shielded. We were told they had been ordered not to fire their weapons unless fired upon.

Before we left the war council meeting room we were informed a plan was being generated to attack *Golden Dragon* to take out the mothership.

The details were classified Top Secret. The admiral warned us all not to mention this to anyone outside the room under threat of castration. The women present were greatly amused.

Attack on the Queen—Captain Hiroshi Koyama

All of New Jerusalem was put on high alert as soon as the simulacrums left the war council meeting. A plan was developed for neutralizing the Hive Queen and it involved a single shuttle launching into an orbit a few hundred miles above *Golden Dragon's* current synchronous orbit over New Jerusalem.

Just before we launched, our crew was standing by our shuttle awaiting final instructions from the admiral. The crew stood at parade rest as he went over the mission one last time. When he finished, he paused for a moment, then said, "Commander Koyama, please step forward."

I took one step forward and came to attention.

"Commander, you are hereby promoted to the rank of captain based on your time in rank as a commander and your outstanding performance in leading critical missions."

From out of nowhere, my wife appeared on the tarmac next to me with silver eagles to pin on my shoulders. She kissed me on the cheek and whispered, "You'd better come back to me, my captain," then stepped back.

In a loud voice, the admiral said, "Shuttle crew, atten…hut! Good hunting. Dismissed."

We all saluted smartly, turned, and boarded our shuttle.

To avoid detection of our shuttle, all of our remaining shuttles were launched at once and set out on recon missions up to a hundred miles from our city center. Their flight patterns were random with altitudes varying from three to ten thousand feet with constant changes in velocity making it more difficult to track them all or to project their flight path. These shuttles were actually scanning for any possible enemy build ups, however their main function was to tie up the Hive Queen's resources while the attack shuttle slipped away.

The attack shuttle, designated Shuttle Quebec, began doing similar search patterns as the other shuttles. After two circuits, when it crossed paths with another shuttle, it went to maximum stealth mode and dropped down to minimum safe altitude. The flight path was low and slow with all electronics shut down to minimize detection. We kept that profile until we believed we were out of range of the mothership's surveillance equipment. We turned north and began accelerating and climbing. When we crossed over the imaginary border with Canada we began our climb to a polar-synchronous orbit. It took almost a day of a multi G climb to arrive at our desired orbit.

Golden Dragon was currently in a geo-synchronous orbit at twenty-two thousand three hundred miles over the Earth in line with New Jerusalem. Shuttle Quebec moved into a polar-synchronous orbit at an altitude of twenty-two thousand five hundred miles, circling the Earth from pole to pole. We programmed an intercept with *Golden Dragon*; ETA was a day before the second coming.

When our paths crossed we made a retro burn and ended up directly above *Golden Dragon*, one hundred fifty miles apart. We continued to run silent with all electronics shut down as we waited for the next phase of our mission.

In preparing for this mission, we made certain assumptions. The first one was we could get into position undetected. We believed our assumptions had been correct. We successfully got into position without the Hive Queen knowing we were there. Part of the assumption was based on the premise there were limited sensors on the top of the mothership. The other part was she was totally focused on what was going on below her in New Jerusalem. One fun sucker suggested she might know we were above her, but didn't consider us a threat.

One new stealth feature was in play now. It was referred to as passive stealth. The nickname of this new approach was invisibility paint. It was a special epoxy that adhered to the bottom of our shuttle. It prevented any surveillance ping from bouncing back to the mothership and revealing our position. It did this by absorbing and defusing the energy of the ping throughout the epoxy.

We waited patiently for something to happen. It seemed like I checked my wrist chrono every few minutes. Time seemed to creep by. After what seem like a week of waiting, really only ten hours, the Hive Queen began launching her shuttles. We counted a total of thirteen leaving the two shuttle bays.

Our passive sensors were picking up a tremendous amount of communications between the mothership and the shuttles. It appeared they were arranging themselves into some geometric pattern as they began their descent.

We prepared for an attack then waited for the signal from the admiral to begin our attack.

The Second Coming–The Apostles Paul and John

The Sanctuary was almost empty as we waited. We were as ready as we could possibly be. We had been praying most of the night for guidance in how to respond to whatever may happen in the next few hours.

Seated in the pews were the members of the war council. Armed protectors stood outside of the sanctuary doors waiting to be called.

Then it began.

Vid coms outside the Temple were pointed upward. It looked as if large white clouds were beginning to form in the sky directly above us. We saw no enemy shuttles, just large, white, puffy clouds. The vid coms began to pick up the sound of voices, many voices. At first it was difficult to understand what the voices were saying, moments later there was no mistaking they were singing, a heavenly choir was singing the praises of our Lord and Savior.

As we continued to watch, we began to see objects within the clouds, growing larger as they came closer. They were people! Hundreds, perhaps thousands, of people dressed in pure white robes descending from the clouds, floating down toward the Temple plaza. In the midst of these people, this heavenly host, was the softly glowing, glorified body of Jesus. He was easy to recognize. He was tall, slender, with brown eyes and long hair down to his shoulders. His facial features were identical to the image painted by ancient European artists. Those famous paintings had no similarity to the appearance of the typical Jewish man from the Middle East. Jewish men were forbidden by scripture to wear their hair long, just as it was forbidden for women to cut their hair short.

His body was covered in dazzling white robes, the purest of the pure. As his feet reached the tiles of the plaza, the singing stopped. It became totally silent as all eyes focused on him. He faced toward the

Temple, raised his arms, stretching them outward until one could almost imagine him hanging on a cross. He opened his hands and the wounds could be seen. He raised his head, looked heavenward and said, in a deep, strong voice, "Today is the day of the Lord, the day of judgment, a time to separate the good from the evil, a time for the good to be transformed into glorified, immortal bodies and live forever in paradise with me and my Father, a time for the wicked to be cast into the lake of fire and burn for all eternity."

He began to walk from the plaza into the Temple as vid bots followed him, capturing his every move. Before he entered the Sanctuary, we saw Admiral Lawrence speak into his wrist com. "Execute Capture The Queen."

The sanctuary doors opened wide and in walked what appeared to be Jesus of Nazareth followed by The Moses and Pastor Luther. After a few steps down the aisle they stopped, turned to look at the empty pews both on the main floor and in the balconies. He turned back to us and said in an angry voice, "Where are my people, my creations, my believers?" The force of his voice was almost overpowering.

Paul responded, "Surely the Son of God, He who knows the end from the beginning, knew they would not be here."

He glared at Paul and replied, "You test me? You doubt I am your savior? You whom I created wants to joust with me?"

John answered, "We don't *doubt* you are the Son of God. We know for a fact you are not. If you were truly God incarnate, you would follow your own sacred scriptures. The Book or Revelation states that every eye would see your second coming. There are many outside of New Jerusalem who have no idea you are here."

John quickly followed before the pretender had a chance to speak again. "We have no doubt you believe you are Jesus and the others believe they are also real. Unfortunately, you are simulacrums, artificial life grown from DNA with intelligence and memories downloaded into you from the organic AI computer system onboard a space ship, thousands of miles above us."

All three stared at us in disbelief, turned and walked up the aisles toward the Sanctuary doors. Before they exited, the creature who claimed to be Jesus, turned and shouted at us. "This is not over. This has just begun. You will all die terrible deaths. It's a pity you chose not to believe in me."

As they exited the Sanctuary they were grabbed by the security team, placed in shackles and taken to temporary holding cells beneath the Temple.

The admiral stood up and said to us, "Well done apostles. The next round is already under way. You need to get to the shelters."

Another Armageddon? —Captain Hiroshi Koyama

We were in our pressure suits ready to begin our attack. Each of us had roughly an hour of air in our tanks and enough pressurized nitrogen for our maneuvering jets to get us to *Golden Dragon* and return with just a ten percent reserve.

When we got the attack order from the admiral, both of the shuttle hatches were opened. We all exited the shuttle and headed down to the forward and aft shuttle bay doors. Another assumption: the doors would be open like they did when we observed them on our previous recon flight. If they weren't open, we were prepared to blow them thereby losing the element of surprise. At least we hoped it would be a surprise if we could slip inside open bar doors.

Both doors were opened wide! The bays completely empty of any shuttles. Another assumption came true: all the shuttles were being used for their attack. Fifty of our troops entered the forward bay, the other fifty in through the aft bay.

A quick search of the bulkheads revealed hatches to the ship's interior. The hatches were not locked. When opened, there was no rush of escaping air. The ship wasn't pressurized. No breathable air was present. That meant no humans on board.

We filed into the ship's interior through both hatches and fanned out to search for the command center. By convention, the command center would be in the forward end of the ship, but this wasn't a conventional ship. We knew we had to search everywhere.

Our orders were to search for the Hive Queen for no more than thirty minutes. If we couldn't locate her, we were to plant explosive charges throughout the ship, return to Shuttle Quebec, and leave orbit. When we'd reached a safe distance, detonate the bombs and win the war. But we really wanted to find the Hive Queen, shut her down, remove her from *Golden Dragon*, then destroy the ship and win the war.

Dr. Sanborn would begin salivating every time he thought about getting the chance to discover how the Hive Queen worked. It would be at least a century more advanced than the computer systems we currently used.

I was getting reports from the admiral that the enemy shuttles had magically appeared and looked like they were positioning themselves for attack. Then they just vaporized our beam tower! We lost all use of the beam.

Following that, one of Dr. Sanborn's IT specialists thought he had discovered the Hive Queen. "Where is she?" I asked excitedly. "Can you shut her down? Do you think you can remove her quickly?"

The specialist shook his head, "No way to remove her. The Hive Queen *is* the ship. It's distributed throughout every part of the ship, but give me ten minutes."

As he plugged several cables into what looked like multiple data ports on one of the bulkheads, alarms began blaring, lights started to flash. I looked at the specialist, "How much longer?"

He answered, "At least five more minutes captain." He studied the readouts on the surface of the suitcase sized box he was holding. "Now four minutes."

Suddenly the alarms stopped blaring and the lights blinked once and went out, plunging the ship into total darkness. The lights on our helmets turned on automatically. "Three minutes," the specialist shouted.

A loud voice was suddenly broadcasted throughout the ship. I was stunned to hear it was in Japanese. It sounded like a young Japanese woman repeating the same message. "*Golden Dragon* will self-destruct in two minutes." Not exactly the same message, "*Golden Dragon* will self-destruct in one minute fifty seconds."

I activated my all-hands channel and yelled, "Abandon ship! Abandon ship now! Return to the shuttle at best possible speed!"

The specialist shouted, "Two minutes!"

The Japanese woman said, "*Golden Dragon* will self-destruct in one minute thirty seconds."

I screamed in Japanese, "What happened to forty seconds?"

I switched my com to broadcast my voice inside of the ship, "Cancel self-destruct now!" I said in Japanese.

"State authorization code for self-destruct."

I had no clue what the code might be. I took a wild guess, "Hiroshima."

"That code is incorrect. *Golden Dragon* will self-destruct in fifty seconds."

The specialist shouted, "One minute. Just one more minute!"

In desperation I yelled, "Reset self-destruct to five minutes."

I waited an eternity, certain I was going to die. All I could think about was Anna and my children.

The specialist yelled, "That's it, captain. I got it all. Let's get out of here before this tub blows."

We backtracked though the ship into the hanger bay. The specialist launched himself through the bay doors and disappeared from sight as he began his trip back to our shuttle. I was ready to follow him when I heard the young woman's voice again. "The self-destruct drill has been terminated. Have a nice day."

As I launched out the bay and headed up to our shuttle, I felt like I had aged ten years in less than an hour. I grumbled to myself, "Not *once* did I hear the word 'drill,' not once."

When I was aboard our shuttle Trish said, "Welcome aboard, captain. All hands accounted for. Orders?"

Before I could answer, Lieutenant Davis shouted, "*Golden Dragon* is preparing to leave orbit, captain! Her bay doors are closing, her propulsion system is powering up!"

"Did all the explosives get installed and armed?" I asked.

"Aye sir. Just waiting for your command," answered our special weapons chief petty officer.

"Give her thirty minutes to clear the area, then detonate all explosives. Give us a ten second countdown," I replied.

"Aye aye captain. A ten second count down it is."

Thirty minutes later we all stood and watched the large vid screen. *Golden Dragon* with her MHD drive at full power was easy to see. The chief petty officer with the detonation switch in his hand began the count down. The entire crew joined in "10, 9, 8, 7, 6, 5, 4, 3, 2, 1 Detonate!" There was a blinding flash followed by what looked like an ancient's fireworks skyrocket exploding with a million little pieces of golden glitter filling the space that use to be the *Golden Dragon*. I thought to myself, *we didn't need the nukes after all.*

It was the middle of the night when we finally touched down at New Jerusalem. Everyone aboard was exhausted after the adrenalin rush had worn off. We just wanted to get to our respective homes. I think most of us expected our families would be waiting for us as we exited the shuttle. We were not prepared for the wall of cheering that greeted us. It seemed like a million floodlights were turned on simultaneously, turning the pitch black of night into blinding white light. I could barely make out the building and hangers that surrounded the landing area.

Suddenly groups of people began running towards the entire shuttle crew. My first thought was one of horror. *Golden Dragon* had won after all. These weren't people running to greet us. These were avatars with battering ram watermelons hiding inside. Some must have been androids ready to pull us apart limb by limb. I didn't even want to imagine the damage the simulacrums could do.

Before I could even raise my hands to defend myself I was engulfed by my family. Anna jumped into my arms and hugged me so tightly I thought she might break one or two of my ribs. My older son was pounding me on the back and I could see tears streaming down his cheeks. My other son had grabbed me around the waist with his face buried against my shoulder. I could feel the wetness of his tears through my flight suit. My youngest, my daughter, had a death grip on my knee, causing my lower leg to go numb as she chanted, "Daddy, Daddy, Daddy."

My emotions changed in a millisecond from stark terror to the incredible happiness of being home safe with those I loved most dearly. I realized, I was getting too old for all of this. I wasn't exactly sure what all this truly was, however I was certain I was getting too old for it.

Summary of the One Day War—The War Council

The war ended quickly, but none of us are sure why the war happened.

At first we thought it was to gain access to the technology in the ancient's lab. However, upon further review of *Golden Dragon* and its Hive Queen computer system, their technology far surpassed anything we had in the lab.

Others thought it was to make us their slaves or perhaps to eliminate all human life and let artificial life reign. We just don't know. Hopefully we will learn more if and when Dr. Sanborn's team of IT experts decipher the data they extracted from *Golden Dragon* before it was destroyed.

Now I want to focus on what happened in New Jerusalem after the three simulacrums were taken prisoners in the Temple. Those three creatures gave me the creeps. Paul and John shared that feeling. To them it seemed surreal to argue with the Lord's replicant. Simon said he knew the synthetic Moses' wasn't real, however, in his heart he *wanted* him to be real. He missed him so much. I think Klaus and his wife felt the same about Pastor Luther.

Once these three were taken prisoner and led away to jail cells in the Temple basement, things changed dramatically. The clouds and the heavenly host vanished to be replaced by *Golden Dragon's* shuttles.

The shuttles formed up into an inline formation. One by one they swooped down, landed briefly, disgorged fifty to one hundred troops, then took off again. There were thirteen shuttles in all, it took about fifteen minutes for all the shuttles to drop off their troops and move back into a ground support role two thousand feet above the Temple plaza.

Analysis of the vids of the battle showed the troops breaking up into squads of nine or ten soldiers, roughly one hundred twenty squads, all with orders to attack specific targets within New Jerusalem.

The strange thing about it was there was no talking. No shouting commands from leaders to grunts. No response of grunts to leaders. Everyone knew exactly where to go and what they were supposed to do when they got there. Nobody ran into each other, it looked like well-rehearsed choreography.

Each troop appeared to be heavily armed as they began to move towards their respective targets, but no shots were fired by either side. I ordered our troops not to fire until fired upon.

As best we can tell, just before the enemy troops prepared to open fire, the Hive Queen's brain was disabled. It is believed the downloading of data by our IT specialist disrupted the orders being transmitted to the enemy troops. As if on cue, all of them fell to the ground unable to move let alone fight. A review of the vids show all one thousand fell within a tenth of a second of each other. There were exceptions. The avatar troops vanished and their respective watermelons fell to the ground along with the android and simulacrum troops.

The shuttles were different. Apparently they had limited autonomous control. When the Hive Queen's signals were interrupted, each shuttle attempted to find a place to land without any coordination between them. That resulted in the destruction of all but two shuttles which landed safely then shut down all systems. Fortunately, none of our people were injured by those crashes, however, several buildings were severely damaged. The Temple survived intact.

Autopsies of the simulacrums revealed that their natural brains had been removed and replaced with organic AI brain constructs.

When the connection with the Hive Queen was broken, all brain function ceased and they all suffocated.

It took almost two weeks to clear the Temple plaza of the debris. Some of the androids and avatar watermelons were kept for experimental purposes as well as the two surviving shuttles. All of the simulacrums were cremated. Their ashes were buried in a large, deep hole. No marker was placed at that spot. They were considered soulless abominations, not humans.

<u>End of the Decade—Commodore Hiroshi Koyama</u>

I can't believe another ten years has gone by. There've been many changes during that time. Several of our leaders have either died or retired. Of course, new people have taken their places. Rear Admiral David Lawrence was promoted by the Tribunal to Vice Admiral (Retired). His promotion was based on his performance in leading us to victory over *Golden Dragon*. The next day he also retired from the Tribunal, claiming he was going to learn how to play golf and play with his grandchildren. His last act was to nominate me as his replacement and promoting me from captain to commodore. In his retirement speech, he said, "It's time for us old war horses to step aside and let the next generation take over."

Captain Henry White was also promoted to commodore. He also retired shortly thereafter. He never fully recovered from his attack by the avatar and her watermelon. He still volunteered at the recreation center. In honor of his sacrifices, the center was renamed the Commodore Henry White Recreation Center and Weight Training Facility. His wife, Dr. Soo Song, continued her Korean martial arts training classes. I've heard it rumored she was also considering stepping down as the head of New Jerusalem's medical centers.

The two Apostles, Paul and John, remained as co-leaders of the New Jerusalem Christian Church. Chaplin George acted as a consultant when needed. There were also a smattering of Jewish Temples and even some Muslim mosques. There were also those who chose not to believe in God. They didn't hold any meetings that I was aware of. Everyone seemed to get along without too much friction. At least there haven't been any religious riots for over a decade.

There have been some significant deaths within our ranks during the last ten years, four as the decade closed. The first to leave us was Governor John Stewart. He died of a heart attack during a Tribunal meeting. He had been the ruler of the civilians when we were aboard the generation ship *Hope,* the last generation returning from Proxima B. He maintained that role after we merged with New Jerusalem. He was always the voice of reason in the most difficult of times.

Marine Major Douglas Fleharty was killed in a training exercise. His small shuttle lost power during a flight maneuver. Four trainees were lost with him.

Healer Johnson, formerly Chief Senior Healer, took her own life. Once she was exposed as collaborating with Judge Aaron in the murder of The Moses a decade ago, she had been scorned by a large part of the New Jerusalem population. Many thought she should have been stoned along with the judge. Her death was ruled death by natural causes, however, her few remaining friends believed she had taken a vial of the same neurotoxin used to assassinate The Moses. Somehow she had hidden it for years. Some say she did it because she couldn't live with the guilt any longer. Confidential medical records revealed she had an inoperable cancerous brain tumor and would have died soon. They claim she took her own life to avoid the pain.

Perhaps the most tragic passing was that of Senior Security Priest Simon. He was one of the first people I met when I was sent down to reconnoiter New Jerusalem. How should I describe our initial relationship? Perhaps the kindest thing to say was we were not close friends. In fact, he wanted to have me executed as a spy. As I recall, The Moses wasn't too fond of me either. He sentenced me to be stoned to death as a heretic along with my future wife, Anna.

Apparently, I didn't make a good first impression.

Simon was once described as a tenacious bulldog. Once he had his mind made up, he seldom changed it. As unlikely as it was, we became great friends and worked closely together on numerous occasions. He was the most loyal man I had ever met. His devotion to

The Moses knew no limits. He would have sacrificed his life in a heartbeat for the man who became our religious leader.

When The Moses died, Simon was the driving force behind the investigation to find the killers. Even after all the evidence pointed at him as the killer, he never gave up. When the real killer was finally determined, tried and executed, he finally stepped back and went on with his life. He became an integral part in our last war.

When the simulacrum of The Moses appeared, Simon changed. He knew the creature who stood before him could not possibly be real, but he wanted him to be. With all his heart he wanted him back. When the Hive Queen ceased to function and the simulacrums died, for Simon it was like losing his leader all over again. Once the war was over, the bodies removed and the carnage cleaned up, he wasn't the same. He was withdrawn, moody, quick to anger over insignificant things. His health began to deteriorate, but he would do nothing to restore it.

On one afternoon, he flew into a rage at one of his subordinates for some inconsequential infraction. The subordinate responded in kind and Simon struck him. He was in the process of striking him a second time when his heart failed.

He was dead before his body hit the floor.

When we heard the news we were all in shock. Many of us were in denial. He couldn't be dead, not now. It took me several days before I accepted the truth. During those days, I found myself picking up my com unit and beginning to contact him before I realized what I was doing. A stab of pain would run through me as I put the com unit back on my desk. The fourth time, after I realized what I was doing, I began to shake. It became uncontrollable. I began to moan, then sob, gut wrenching sobs followed by cries of anguish. I was in my Tribunal office when this happened. Fortunately, so was Dr. Song. She ran into my office with a small bag in hand. I was trying to stand and she grabbed me, pulled me into a hug to keep me from falling to the floor. I kept yelling, "He's gone. He's really gone. Oh my God, he's really gone."

I felt a slight pinch as Soo placed the injector against my neck and pulled the trigger. Almost instantly, the anguish left me, unfortunately, so did my strength. Soo half carried, half drug me to a couch and laid me down as I drifted off to la la land.

When I awoke, Anna was there holding my hand. Soo asked, "How are you feeling now?"

"Foolish," I answered, "But better. Thank you, doctor." I tried to sit up, didn't have the strength and asked, "What did you give me?"

The doctor smiled and said, "An elephant tranquilizer. It seems to have produced the desired effect. Just lie quietly until it wears off. Just so you know, you aren't the only one going through this kind of reaction. I had to tranquilize Dr. Sanborn and the subordinate Simon was arguing with. You should be better now. You'll still be sad, that's the normal reaction to grieving for someone you're close to. I don't think you will have any further denial episodes. Just in case, I'll keep a loaded injector in my office. Scream if you need me."

A few days later, we all attended Simon's funeral. The service was limited to his close friends. He wasn't married, except to his work, however, he had many friends. He had been the Godfather of my first born. I was surprised at how at peace I felt. I wondered if most of the grieving process was over for me, or if I was still feeling the effects of the elephant tranquilizer.

The next day a new SSP was appointed by the Tribunal. She was an outstanding candidate, exceptionally well qualified with ten years of experience. She had also earned the rank of second degree black belt from my school before defecting to take Soo Song's self-defense classes. Soo also voted for her. The twins made it unanimous. They had seen her at church on numerous occasions and she had attended the Bible study classes on the Ten Commandments.

It was our combined opinion she was just what we needed for the new SSP position. Her name was Deanna Lawrence.

<u>Looking Ahead—Commodore Hiroshi Koyama</u>

What will the next decade bring?

If the last two were the norm we can expect the unexpected.

There are a lot of questions left over which need answers. A great many of them are focused on *Golden Dragon* and her proposed mission. Let me give a few examples: Did she ever go to Proxima B? If she did why did she return to Earth? Her mission plan had her delivering three thousand humans to the colony, along with fertilized embryos. Then she was to be dismantled and her parts taken down to the planet's surface to build more infrastructure. However, when our troops invaded the ship, they didn't find any cryo-sleep chambers or any provisions for sustaining human life. There was no life support equipment discovered that would be necessary after the humans were resuscitated. Was her mission changed, if so, by whom?

One interesting theory involves the organic computer system. When it came online, it became sentient. It became the Hive Queen and if she decided she didn't like the original mission, she could have changed it. Changed it to what? Was she exterminating all human life on Earth to finish what The Plague had begun?

When I spoke to Dr. Sanborn about all this, he shrugged and said, "I have no idea at this point. However, once we decode the data we extracted from the Hive Queen maybe we will have answers to some of those questions."

"When can we expect to have the data decoded?" I asked.

He shrugged again and answered, "Who knows? Maybe a few years, maybe another decade. This technology is a century more advanced than anything we have ever seen. It's hard to predict when we will get results."

Another area of questions concerns the Proxima B colony. We have bits and pieces of transmissions from the colony. Remember, it takes four years for a message to reach us from the colony and another four to reply. Most of the time the signals seem to fade in and out leaving large gaps in the information.

It seems from the messages we received in the past the colony was doing well. There had been a steady growth in the population. There had not been any negative reactions to the local flora and the weather patterns had been as predicted. They made no mention of *Golden Dragon* arriving which would seem to indicate she never made it to the colony, or perhaps they arrived but left unexpectedly.

The colony must have recently made some significant upgrades to their equipment because the last message from them was crystal clear. They said they discovered indigenous life on the planet, intelligent life. They were having limited success communicating with the new life form. We received that message almost a year ago. We haven't heard anything since then.

Of course, this caused quite a reaction from all of us in New Jerusalem. Everyone wanted to know what the alien species looks like, how intelligent are they, are they friendly, are they flesh eating monsters, do they have souls?

The last question caused much discussion.

The twin Apostles were very busy researching the scriptures to give a proper answer. They said the Bible speaks of other intelligent beings that were created prior to the creation of man. They were spread throughout the universe. These beings were more intelligent than man, at least temporarily. There were also Biblical references to different types of these creatures. Some were considered to be good, but there were also bad ones.

They could not find a scriptural reference that these creatures had souls, however it did say they were immortal which might imply they had souls. It came as no surprise these creatures were called angels and demons. That led to the question of whether the aliens on

Proxima B were the good angels or were they the bad demons. Or perhaps they were neither. They could be a completely different species of alien which took us back to the original question, do they have souls? Finally, the Apostles had to say they didn't know, but they were open to discuss all opinions. That was probably the wrong thing to say, they were inundated by hundreds of suggestions, some thought provoking, others totally absurd. A month later everyone had moved on to other things to keep themselves amused.

The IT people suggested sending a message to the colony asking what they did to improve their communication. Our people believe they had some promising ideas for including video. If it worked, in eight short years we could have vids of the intelligent aliens.

In addition to the above, I'm sure new challenges will arise we can't even begin to image. We hope and pray they don't include any more wars or natural disasters. It would be so nice to have a normal boring life for a few years, just to catch our breath. Maybe I could learn to play golf and how to hit the little ball into the little cup.

Anna just comm'd me and said we are going to be grandparents. Boy do I feel old, but life is good. May God continue to bless us all.

The End

About the Author:

Frank G. Davis

Frank is a long time resident of Arizona. He moved from Oregon in 1965 to attend graduate school at Arizona State University. After earning his Master of Science degree in Engineering, he began his professional career as an engineer at a local aerospace company designing gas turbine engines. After 22 years as an engineer, he received an MBA and became a sales manager for the Allied-Signal Corporation. This new position provided the opportunity to travel extensively to numerous Asian and European countries. He retired in 2001 after 36 years of service.

During those 36 years he also became a commercial pilot and flight instructor, a power lifter, and earned black belts in three different styles of martial arts. He continues to train and has reached the level of San Dan in Shotokan Karate. He was also an Assistant Professor at the College of Engineering at ASU for a year.

Since retirement he and his wife of 45 years, Alicia, have become very active in their church. Recently, he began to return to writing, mostly science fiction, a hobby that he dabbled in off and on for most of his life. Several things happened that led to this novel: a series of inspirational sermons, ideas for stories that "popped into his head," and the corona virus pandemic which restricted him to his house. He figured he might as well get serious about writing.

Enjoy all the works of Frank G. Davis
Available in both paperback and ebook

Future Histories
Four short stories from the future
1. **Real**
2. **The Elect**
3. **Zombie Pilgrims**
4. **Stephen**

Professor Radcliff's Time Machine

A university professor takes his students on a wild ride through time from an ancient Pharaoh to the end of the world.

The first two books of the Generations Trilogy

Join the crew of the generation ship *Hope* as they return from Alpha Centauri to find the world decimated by a plague. See how they join with Earth's survivors to build a new civilization. The last book of the trilogy will be released in February, 2021.

For more information on these books, go to:

scififrank.com